New *X Rated* titles from *X Libris*:

The *X Libris* series:

Wicked Ways

Zara Devereux

X RATED

An *X Libris* Book

First published in Great Britain in 2001
by X Libris

A CIP catalogue record for this book
is available from the British Library.

ISBN 0 7515 3109 X

Typeset by
Derek Doyle & Associates, Liverpool
Printed and bound in Great Britain by
Clays Ltd, St Ives plc

X Libris
A Division of
Little, Brown and Company (UK)
Brettenham House
Lancaster Place
London WC2E 7EN

www.littlebrown.co.uk

Wicked Ways

Chapter 1

'*IT'S A SORRY STATE* of affairs when someone like me – talented, educated and drop-dead gorgeous – can't get a job,' Kelly said ironically, striding about the kitchen. 'Thank God I don't have to pay rent. The council tax is enough to cope with, to say nothing of gas and electric, and all the other bills that seem to plop through the letterbox with depressing regularity. I'm thinking of going on the game, becoming a lady of absolutely no repute.'

'It's the same for me,' Judith replied. 'I thought when I finished college they'd all be clamouring to recruit me for high-powered posts. But zilch. The employment office staff is helpful, but keep offering me shelf-stacking in supermarkets, or waitressing. Which I wouldn't mind short-term, but it isn't exactly what I slogged hard for ... I got decent grades in history and literature.'

'And you don't want to go on and take a teaching course?'

'I certainly don't,' Judith replied with a shudder. 'Imagine trying to control a class of spotty oiks oozing testosterone, and girls who tart themselves up as potential jail-bait. No thank you!'

1

Kelly smiled across at her friend. They had known each other for years, starting primary school at the same time – that neat and efficient little church establishment in a West Country village. They'd also shared secondary education, going by bus to the nearest comprehensive, there to follow their natural creative bents and, more importantly, to get a basic training in the wide and never-to-be reconciled difference between males and females.

But Judith was always the shy one, Kelly mused, refilling their cups with instant coffee. Me? I've never been able to keep my gob shut, always had too much to say for myself. As for the lads – I did my fair share of showing them mine behind the bike shed. They seemed impressed . . . but I can't say I thought much of *theirs*. The cock is a strange object. I thought so then and I still do now.

She was feeling particularly irritable that morning. The post had brought disconcerting news and she didn't quite know how to handle it. She pushed the letter across the table towards Judith. 'It's the latest concerning my darling mama,' she said, pretending to turn it into a joke, though hurting inside. 'There's good news and bad news. Which d'you want to hear first?'

'I don't mind,' Judith answered, staring at her, blue eyes wide behind her steel-framed spectacles.

Kelly was tempted to ask her why she didn't do something about those plain-Jane glasses. But then, Judith had never bothered much about her looks – skinny where Kelly was slim; hunched-shouldered, as if ashamed of her figure, while Kelly held herself proudly, breasts thrust out. And her dull, mousy hair was completely lacking in style, combed back and fastened with a slide.

'Read it for yourself,' Kelly said, then, without

2

waiting for her to do so, added angrily, 'She's only gone and got herself pregnant, that's all! Had me when she was eighteen, then nothing. Now she's run off with her toy-boy – who is younger than me – and announces that she's up the duff! Jesus Christ, I shall be twenty-four by the time it's born. What an age to have a new brother or sister! Well done, Mother. You always did know how to screw everything up.'

'I think it's rather sweet,' said Judith, and handed back the letter. 'If only something like that had happened to my parents ... But they've stuck together, though they row like cat and dog. I was so glad when Daddy's firm sent him to Australia and they went over there for good. And I never see my brother, Robert. He doesn't bother to keep in touch, although there's only him and me. He was always their favourite. I was never an achiever like him, though they tried to force me into it. I couldn't come up to their expectations. Robert did brilliantly, of course.'

'But you got to uni.'

'I know. And my results weren't half bad.'

'There you are then. Be proud of yourself,' Kelly said, adding, 'Families are a pain.'

She shrugged, then ran a hand through her tousled chestnut mane. The curls coiled round her fingers, natural and bouncy and, she thought, incredibly boring. What could you do with hair that grew like a bush, stubbornly twisted itself into corkscrew ringlets and refused to be tamed? Have a crop-cut and get rid of it, she had almost decided on more than one occasion.

'Exactly,' Judith agreed.

'Oh, well, according to the rest of this, her meeting Andy-baby has done me a power of good,' Kelly continued. 'Dad had decamped with his secretary anyway, so I suppose you can't really blame Mother for grabbing at happiness. The *good* news is that she's written to say she's signed this cottage over to me. Grandma left it to her. And now that she's split from my father and bought a wine bar in Spain, she says I'm to look on it as mine. Willing to sign over the deeds. They won't be coming back and the baby's to be born in Malaga.'

'You're lucky,' Judith murmured, huddled on the stool, her dun-coloured cardigan hunched round her, legs hidden under a long tweed skirt, the heels of her sensible brown lace-up shoes hitched on the lower rung. 'I'm staying with Mrs Tanner ... you know, Mum and Dad's neighbour. She was recruited to look after me. Wish I was still at university.'

'So do I,' Kelly agreed enthusiastically. 'All those blokes – it was wicked!'

'I wasn't thinking about them. I just loved studying.'

'I know. You're barking. Do you love Peter, too? Does he float your boat?'

Judith flushed, and the colour suited her. Kelly thought: I really must take her in hand – not literally, of course – well, not *yet*, though it might be fun to introduce her to lesbian love ... I'm lucky to be bi-sexual; I get the best of both worlds. But just for now she needs me to teach her about make-up. A touch of blusher would work wonders on that dull skin.

'Peter's OK,' Judith said, fiddling with the sleeves of her cardigan. 'I've known him for years.'

'Haven't we all, dear,' Kelly said tartly. 'He's a good guy, but about as exciting as watching paint dry. What's he like in the trouser department? Have you fucked him?'

She didn't really think Judith had, and would have put money on her being a virgin, so it came as a shock and confirmed her theory that you never really know a person, no matter how much of a bosom-buddy, when Judith said, 'Yes.'

'Oh? When?' Kelly felt outraged suddenly, as if a younger sister had confided that she'd been lap-dancing. In fact, that was just how she saw Judith, even though they were the same age – as a non-streetwise sibling who needed looking after.

'When I got back home from uni. I was lonely. Though I didn't get on with my parents, there was a huge hole when they'd gone. They grudgingly invited me to go to Sydney, but I refused. Peter stepped in. He was kind . . . supportive. So was his mother. I think she views me as a prospective daughter-in-law.'

'But that's not what you want?' Kelly asked, sitting with her legs apart on the stool opposite Judith.

She was wearing blue jeans so tight that they cut into her labia and the deep crease between her bottom cheeks. She liked the sensation, wriggling a little to drag the seam in deeper, chafing her clitoris. It was early in the year and cold, even though the kitchen was heated by a shiny red enamelled Aga. A big, sloppy sweater topped the T-shirt that covered her breasts. She could feel her nipples becoming erect, rubbed by the underwired lace and satin bra that supported those full globes.

I could do with a man, she thought. It's been a mite too long since I had a stiff dick inside me. But the talent is limited in this one-horse town. Castleford is OK for tourists, and fine for those who commute from London or have lived in the place all their lives. But it's not exactly conducive to wild flings and orgies.

It was different when she'd had a temporary job as

a garage mechanic. Then there were plenty of men: wealthy customers who had wanted to take her out to dinner, with all that that entailed, and fellow grease monkeys in grubby overalls who didn't say no to a grapple in the back of the workshop. This halcyon state of affairs was short-lived, and ended when the boss's wife caught him in the inspection pit. Kelly was with him and he was inspecting more than the under-seal of a Punto.

Now she was poor, jobless and fed up. So, apparently, was Judith, despite having Peter.

'I know,' she said suddenly. 'Move in with me. You can do that, now it's mine. There's bags of room. Are you up for it?'

'But what about Mrs Tanner?'

'Screw Mrs Tanner. You're a big girl now. We can do it properly. Halve the expenses and you won't have to pay rent as I don't even have a mortgage to find. It'll be a blast. We'll look for work together. You can have Peter here overnight – but I don't want him moving in.'

'Of course not. I . . . I wouldn't dream of im . . . imposing . . .' Judith stammered, wringing her hands together nervously. 'I'm not sure I want him, anyway.'

'Doesn't he satisfy you?' Kelly asked bluntly. 'In my experience few men know how to do this properly.'

'I'm not sure I know what you mean,' Judith muttered.

'Do you climax? Does he bring you off? Is it better than when you masturbate?' Kelly plunged on.

'I don't know . . . I mean . . . I never . . .'

'Play with yourself? I don't believe that for a moment. Everyone does.' Kelly was nonplussed, but it didn't stop her gabbling on. 'Is he a caring lover? I mean, does he rub you all over with aromatic oils, kiss your toes, your

6

ears, the nape of your neck, then go down on you, licking your clit and slurping at your fanny.'

Judith's head sank lower, her straight hair falling forward over her flaming cheeks. 'No. He doesn't do any of those things,' she muttered.

'Then it's time he did,' Kelly announced, wanting to rush off and tell Peter exactly what she thought of his lousy lovemaking. 'I can't stand bad manners in bed. I'll bet the world's greatest lovers weren't necessarily handsome, but they knew how to please women . . . had got their diplomas in clitology. That's what really counts, knowing how to treat the clit. It's not the size of their tool, or the length of time they can go on humping, but their skilful use of fingers and mouth on a woman's most sensitive organ.'

'Is that right? I don't know much about sex,' Judith confessed.

'Haven't you ever had an orgasm?'

'I'm not sure.'

'Not sure? That means you haven't or you'd be bloody well sure. There's nothing like it. A mind-blowing sensation, and so easy to produce for yourself. When I'm in the middle of a wank, I often think to myself: who needs men?'

'What about love?' Judith ventured timidly.

'*What about love?*' Kelly repeated mockingly. 'I've been there, done that, got the T-shirt to prove it. Love hurts. Love makes you vulnerable. Love puts you at the mercy of your beloved, allowing them to use, manipulate and control you. I don't do love.'

'I always thought it would be wonderful to fall in love,' Judith said wistfully.

'Hang around with me, girl, and I'll educate you,' Kelly promised, jumping up from the stool and asking, 'When can you move in? Today? Right now?'

'I'll have to let Mrs Tanner know. And there's my laundry part done, and Peter to tell.'

'We can do it all this afternoon. You haven't a lot of gear, have you?' Kelly sprang into action, rummaging in her bag for her car keys. 'Come on, I'll take you in Tracy. We can load everything in the back. Then you can phone Peter and ask him over this evening. I shan't be here, I've arranged to go to a gig at Salisbury Arts Centre with Caroline and Sally. We're on the pull. I'll be back late, so don't wait up for me.'

'All right. Gosh, am I really going to live with you?' Judith's face lit up and Kelly noticed how pretty she became when animated.

'You are. And we'll have a ball. Do all kinds of stuff,' Kelly promised, and rushed Judith through the front door. There, at the kerb, stood the faithful though flighty red Metro, christened Tracy.

They bundled into her and headed up the high street towards the more recently developed end of town where stood Mrs Tanner's neat detached house. The gardens were immaculate, cars washed and polished every Sunday morning and, had lace curtains still been in fashion, they would have twitched when Kelly hove into view on the horizon.

Judith unpacked the last of her cases and stashed her clothes in the wardrobe and chest-of-drawers. Boxes of books were stowed in a cupboard under the eaves, and her portable stereo, CDs and audio tapes placed on a low table near the double bed. Judith had stayed at the cottage before, but only as a guest, never dreaming it would one day be her home.

The bedroom was large and had a sloping ceiling, and tiny dormer windows almost at floor level. The cottage had to be three hundred years old, its bulging stone walls several feet thick, its roof thatched and its main room boasting an inglenook fireplace. There was even the remains of a bread oven and panelling and rafters and that smell which Judith associated with dust and age.

No ghosts, she thought. She hoped not, anyway. It was daunting to think that Kelly wouldn't be there on her first night, but she had already contacted Peter on his cell phone and he had sounded eager to come round and keep her company. She assumed that he would bring a packet of condoms and expect to indulge in a quick shag. Suddenly she realised she was adopting Kelly's way of thinking and talking, using expressions she would have been far too self-conscious to voice once upon a time.

'I'm off now. Will you be all right?' Kelly shouted, seductive perfume wafting up the stairs and tantalising Judith's nostrils as she leaned over the oak banister rail.

'I'll be OK. I'm going to take a shower, and Peter's due at eight,' she said.

'Help yourself to whatever you need. There are cans of lager in the fridge and spare johnnies on my bedside table. OK? If you want incense, there are packets there too. Just watch the candles. The roof's made of straw, remember.'

'I'll be careful.'

The outer door closed and Judith heard Tracy revving up. Now she was alone. She shivered slightly and thought about Mrs Tanner. She hadn't been too pleased, making remarks such as, 'I promised your mother I'd keep an eye on you. Does she know about this? Oh, well, if that's what you want . . . I must say it strikes me as a little ungrateful and selfish, Judith, it really does. After all I've tried to do for you.'

If it hadn't been for Kelly, unmoved and solidly packing up Judith's belongings, she would probably have capitulated and stayed. But there was a steely look in Kelly's green eyes, and a determined set to her mouth that had alarmed Judith more than Mrs Tanner's snide remarks and offishness.

I'm free! The idea was intoxicating. There was no one she need answer to. Kelly was a breeze compared to people of Mrs Tanner's ilk, who had always managed to boss her about.

And I'm sure I'll get work soon, she thought, confidence soaring. Then I'll be really independent.

She watched her full-length reflection in the pierglass as she unbuttoned her blouse and hung it over the back of a pink Lloyd Loom chair. She had removed her glasses, and could see reasonably well without them, except when reading. It was as if she hid behind them, hoping they gave her a more scholarly look, and concealed her true feelings from a hostile world. At least, she had felt it to be hostile for as long as she could remember.

Without them, her true features emerged: heart-shaped face, with a short nose and pointed chin. Her eyes were cornflower blue, her brows arched and well defined. She grabbed a handful of hair and lifted it high, twisting it into a coronet at the top of her head. The transformation was startling, giving her a regal appearance.

Standing taller, she arched her neck and pulled in her ribs. Her breasts stood out, small though they were and enclosed in a white cotton sports bra that did nothing for uplift and separation. But I look almost attractive, she concluded.

She hadn't been telling the truth when Kelly asked her if she played with herself. She did, of course. It would have been unlikely for her to have reached her twenties without discovering the joys of masturbation. But she didn't often indulge, only when the feeling built up unbearably, demanding to be relieved. This often happened after Peter had been with her, his inept lovemaking stoking her passions but never satisfying them. She was always ashamed of herself afterwards, though.

But now, senses roused by the move and the anticipation of an exciting new life, she cupped her breasts in her hands and permitted her thumbs to revolve on the hardening nipples. They responded immediately, rising under the white cotton. She rubbed them simultaneously, feeling pleasure radiate down to her pussy.

The sight of herself in the mirror was arousing, too. Gone was the timid creature who had always lacked an escort at Student Union functions. This girl looked wild and wanton, eyes heavy-lidded with lust, mouth parted over even teeth, tongue tip moistening her full, sensual lips. She watched that tongue, so pink and wet, and brooded on the idea of cunnilingus, something she'd read about in books but never tried. She imagined she'd be far too shy to let someone lick her most private place, yet hot waves of longing tingled through her as she wondered what it would feel like, and her clitoris throbbed and juice trickled from her opening in far greater abundance than when Peter caressed her.

I'm perverted, she panicked. This can't be normal – can it?

Normal or not, she let her fantasies run riot as she lowered her hand and scrunched up her skirt, raising it above her knicker line. In the mirror, she saw that tantalising triangle emerge, a V of pure white that hid her pubic floss. Not as white as it should be, she thought, as

11

she glimpsed a stain following the line of her slit, and felt it too, wet and sticky. Thank goodness there was no chance of Mrs Tanner finding this evidence of her depravity in the laundry basket. She had been certain that the woman examined her underwear. Now no one should touch it but herself. Peter could ejaculate all over her panties and no one would be any the wiser. And not only Peter . . . there might be others.

She was getting hotter now, thinking about the men who would want to fuck her. Always one to indulge in unbridled imaginings, she had peopled her dream-world with swashbuckling heroes plucked straight from romantic historical novels, wearing tight breeches, velvet doublets, and wielding swords. Lately, having seen the latest epic about gladiators, she had reverted to fantasies associated with Ancient Rome and the combat in the arena, all blood, savagery and sun-browned male flesh. She had studied this period avidly, not so much to gain insight into the mighty empire, but simply because the men looked so marvellously sexy in short tunics and armour, greaves and wristbands.

Not much likelihood of meeting someone like that in Castleford, she reflected ruefully. Better to keep my rape fantasies to myself. It wasn't real rape that she fanta-sised about, of course. She didn't want to be forced by a stranger with a power complex, but rather by the man her mind had chosen. Try as she might, Peter got in the way when he entered her physically, and she found it hard to concentrate on her dream lover.

Not now, however, when she was about to give in to the urge to satisfy herself.

She closed her eyes and sighed. Her fingers crept under her panties and combed through her sparse brown bush. Then she hitched her thumbs into the

12

elasticated waist and eased them down and off. She could smell her own rich, oceanic odour, and slid her favourite pussy finger into her slippery avenue. Entering her love-channel was fine – two fingers, three – but after working them in and out, she withdrew and gently annointed the source of all delight – the swelling bud of her clitoris.

She parted her legs, bracing herself and thrusting her pelvis forward, chasing the sensation as her finger massaged each side of that ardent little organ, then centred just above its head, using a circular motion. It was delaying, tormenting, glorious – she was making her clit wait, prolonging the moment until she finally succumbed and rubbed herself to ecstasy.

In her head she was acting out a scenario. She had watched Marcus take part in the gladiatorial games in the circus that afternoon. He was lucky. Still alive. She had determined to have him. He had been triumphant and she had ordered that he be brought to her, a wealthy Roman lady used to being obeyed, married to a senator who was much more interested in slender-limbed young men than herself. Marcus had arrived, so handsome close up that her cunt had clenched and her pulse had raced. Still sweaty from combat, blood smeared his arms and torso. He had been pitted against a tiger and, this vanquished, his next opponent had been a man armed with trident and net. Again, he had triumphed and the crowd had roared for him. He was the hero of the hour. The Emperor had graciously awarded him the laurel wreath, and Judith had sent round to invite him to her villa.

She had fed him and given him wine, then, unable to delay while he bathed, had urged him, dirty, bloody and perspiring, to her bedchamber. Now he lay with her on her silken couch, and his rough, calloused palms stroked her body through the diaphanous cream robe that barely concealed her. He was unexpectedly gentle, his dark eyes smiling at her as he kissed her all over – her gold-sandalled feet, her perfumed calves, thighs and belly, pushing aside her gown, nuzzling her breasts. She was smeared with blood from the wounds inflicted by the tiger's claws. She could smell that feline creature. Its acrid odour mingled with the strong male scent of him, the sweat of exertion, the adrenaline that had pumped through his muscles, the musky odour of his genitals. She inserted a hand under his short linen tunic and ran her hand over his huge erection and heavy balls, barely contained by a loincloth.

Judith moaned with pleasure, glimpsing herself in the mirror in Kelly's cottage, yet at the same time in Rome in the arms of Marcus. She felt hot inside, her fingers slipping in and out, her thumb pressing on her clitoris, his imaginary mouth caressing both, his tongue filling her like a fleshy penis, then jabbing at her clit, lips sucking, sucking . . .

She lifted one foot and placed it on the dressing-table stool. From that angle she could see her sex stretching from clit to anus, wet and glistening. She imagined Marcus looking at her, and this increased her excitement. She rammed two fingers inside herself and worked them around, aping the movements of coitus. This wasn't enough to give her the ultimate pleasure. She withdrew her fingers and spread them so that two held back her labial wings, then she used her middle digit to stroke her clitoris that stood out proud, red and throbbing.

Forgetting Marcus and Peter and even herself, she concentrated on massaging that eager sliver of flesh. Her nipples protruded, lifting the cotton bra. She

14

hurriedly pushed down one of the shoulder straps and freed a breast, pinching and pulling at the rose-pink teat. Excitement speared her, mainlining with her needful clit, and sharp cries of pleasure escaped from her throat. She was about to come. She could feel the hot waves roaring through her body, from her toes to her cortex. Then she was swept high, lifted to the stars, in the grip of a fierce climax.

Gradually she came down from the heights. Marcus saluted and strode off in the direction of the bath. She would join him there soon. She had just bought him from the banker, Tiberio, freeing him from thraldom where he risked his life daily, and making him her love-slave ... Then reality broke through her sensual encounter. Someone was knocking on the front door.

After hurriedly wiping her sticky fingers, she dragged on her panties, skirt and blouse and went downstairs.

'It's all right, Judith. It's only me,' Peter shouted from outside.

She let him in, hoping he wouldn't be able to smell the taint of sex that must cling to her crack and fingers. Even washing never quite got rid of that penetrating, persistent aroma.

She gave herself a mental shake. This was *Peter*, one of the kindest, most gentle men she knew. He'd be terribly upset if he realised that he never satisfied her and that she invented strong, even brutal lovers as an aid to masturbation. She knew she should tell him, but didn't know how to start. It was hard to explain, even to the most caring of partners, what you wanted them to do to bring you to completion. So embarrassing, in fact, that she couldn't do it.

'Come in,' she said, standing back so that he might enter. 'Kelly's out.'

'So we're alone?' he asked, with a quirky grin. 'You going to show me your bedroom, then?'

She wanted to say no, annoyed by his assumption, but it was impossible. She was too used to pleasing people.

'If you like,' she said, and led the way, too ashamed of what she had just done to say that she'd rather sit in the kitchen and have a cup of tea with him before proceeding to more intimate matters.

She was silly, she supposed, for Peter was a pleasant-looking man, with a craggy face, pale blue eyes and fair hair that flopped over his forehead. Compactly built, he was just under six foot tall, and kept his body in trim by jogging and playing football. Absolutely reliable, he had his own business making handcrafted furniture, and orders were increasing weekly, mostly from abroad. At the moment, he lived with his widowed mother, but he had already intimated that soon he'd be buying a house of his own and wanted Judith to share it with him – as his wife.

'You've done well for yourself there,' Mrs Tanner had remarked, when she got wind of this. 'You'll need someone to help you prepare for the wedding. I don't mind offering my services.'

'We're not even engaged. He hasn't asked me properly yet,' Judith had replied, outraged by the woman's pushy attitude. What with her and Peter's mother dropping heavy hints, it was enough to put a girl off marriage for life.

It seemed that he was delighted with the new arrangements. He stopped on the stairs and pulled Judith into his arms, kissing her soundly. She could feel his cock rising against her belly, and responded to that urgent pressure. The cottage enfolded them in secretive stillness, and she thought that maybe this was what they had needed. They'd never made love in a bed. Their only opportunities to do it had been in the back of Peter's car or in the woods, and on one occasion on the settee in his mother's house when she was at a WI meeting. Judith had always been afraid they'd be discovered and this had inhibited her.

Maybe that's why I haven't been able to come with him, she thought, as her lips relaxed and her tongue tangled with his in a dance of desire. I need privacy in order to let myself go. She could feel excitement building up in her loins, her nipples hardening and her vagina aching for something hard and large to clench around. She closed her eyes, lying back in Peter's embrace, his tongue exploring her teeth and the delicate inner membranes of her mouth. *This time* they'd achieve that simultaneous orgasm which she'd heard was the be-all and end-all of human coupling.

'Wow!' Peter removed his mouth from hers long enough to exclaim. 'You should have moved before if it meant you'd be so hot for me.'

She released herself, and, fingers linked with his, led him into her room. There she urged him to lie on the bed while she undressed for him. This, too, was a first. She let her blouse slide off, then unzipped her skirt. It slithered to the floor. She was a little embarrassed by the unadorned white garter belt that held up her stockings, but one look at Peter's engrossed expression assured her that he had no qualms about such simple, girlish underwear. She unclipped the suspenders and rolled down the stockings, then took the belt off, each movement one of tantalising slowness.

All she wore now were her panties and bra. It was odd to be so shy in front of the man who had taken her

17

virginity – a painful experience as she recalled, and certainly not the high she had been led to expect through misinformation gleaned from romance stories.

She felt suddenly wanton. Peter seemed hypnotised, his hand straying to the thick baton of flesh rising hard behind his fly front. His enslavement empowered her. She could do anything she liked with him while he was controlled by his lust. Moving sensuously, as if to an internal rhythm, she gyrated her hips, reached up and cupped her breasts, then unhooked her bra at the back. The cups eased forward, but the straps kept them in place until she was ready to reveal her treasures to him.

'Oh, Judith,' he whispered, and reached for her, but she pushed him away.

'Naughty,' she scolded, still fingering her nipples. 'I didn't say you could touch.'

With a sudden gesture, she bared her breasts, holding the bra in her fingertips before casting it aside. As if unable to control himself, Peter unbuttoned his trousers and lifted his cock from fly front and boxer shorts. Judith looked at it boldly, no longer reticent, admiring the stubby stem rising from its nest of wiry hair, and concentrating on the bare helm. It looked so vulnerable, though huge and fiery red, its slit shining with dew.

Peter held it and said, 'I want to put it in you.'

'I'll bet you do,' she teased, then turned her back on him, pulled down her knickers and bent over from the waist, exposing her arse and letting her hips bump and grind. She couldn't see him, but she heard his groan and the rapid friction of his palm racing over his cock.

She removed her knickers and, turning to face him,

18

threw them at him. They landed over his nose, a silky bundle carrying traces of her pussy juice. Peter groaned again as he breathed in.

'Jesus God!' he cried, his voice muffled, 'I can smell your cunt.'

This was the moment to tell him he could get even closer to it – she could boldly sit on his face and have him lick her out – but Judith didn't quite have the bottle. Instead, she went over to him and pushed him down on the bed. He looked up at her with passion-drugged eyes, then reared up so that he was on top, and from that minute on, Judith knew she wasn't going to orgasm.

It was like every time before. He lay on her, kissed her, tweaked her breasts and then left her long enough to roll on a condom. Back in position, he kneed her thighs apart, introduced his latex-covered prick to her wet crack and pushed hard, lodging it inside her. He sighed, drew it out, then thrust it back in again. At no time did his cock or its base rub against her clit. He might just as well have been a mile away for all the good it did her.

Struggling with disappointment, Judith wriggled and heaved, though this was difficult as he insisted on lying on her, squashing her flat. Somewhere in her brain she heard Kelly saying in her no-nonsense voice, 'Gentlemen take their weight on their knees and never, never use their partners as a mattress. It's a no-no.'

'Tell him,' Judith's alter-ego shouted. 'Say to him, "Get off me, you dork! I can't breathe. I'll never come, even if you go on pounding for a hundred years."'

She couldn't do it, but she gave up trying to enjoy it or even pretending that she did. She lay there like a stone while he humped and panted his way to completion and, when he at last grew still, his head buried in

19

her shoulder, she wanted nothing so much as to push him away.

A little vignette lit up her mind. Marcus was in the sunken bath, waiting for her. He leaned back against the tiled side. The black hair was wet and matted on his tanned chest, scrawling down passed his navel and joining the thicket covering his lower belly. His cock rose from the water, a stiff, fleshy rod, and his balls floated beneath it.

Peter withdrew from her, rolled on his side and started to snore. Judith lost herself in her dream, letting her flimsy white robe drop to the lapis lazuli tiles as she stepped into the bath alongside Marcus . . .

Chapter 2

'*THERE'S NOWHERE TO BLOODY* park!' Kelly shouted, steering Tracy round the back of the church at speed.

Deconsecrated, it was now Salisbury Arts Centre, a venue for bands both local and renowned, for plays and concerts and entertainment. One thing's for sure, Kelly thought, I'd never have set foot in it while it was being used for its original purpose. Like love, I don't do churches. I'm a pagan.

'God, you're wired!' complained Sally, her hair all colours of the rainbow in the street-lights, short, spiked and streaked with green, purple, blonde and blue. Too young to be a firstwave punk, she had latched on to its most recent revival. She even had a safety pin in her ear.

'Yeah, take it easy. If I'd thought, I could have borrowed my grandmother's disabled person's parking disc,' added Caroline from the back. Her sleekly elegant appearance covered a well of depravity that Kelly had only just begun to plumb.

'We use that and get caught, I'll get fined a thousand quid,' she answered. 'The car park's rubbish. We'll have to find a side street.'

'But it'll be so far to walk, and I'm breaking in these new shoes,' Sally whined.

'You can just put up or piss off,' Kelly barked, a little resentful. She was the only one with a car, so it was her job to stay sober and act the chauffeur.

The entrance to the church was already heaving and she drove round to the side. There she spotted a couple of men she knew. They were humping gear from the back of a truck, roadies for the headline band, StingRayz. It was her intention to fuck the lead singer who was very pretty and looked like a surfer. She screeched to a halt in a space close by.

'Hi,' said one of them.

His head was shaved and he had a spider tattooed at the back. Gold rings glinted in his eyebrows, nose and lower lip. Kelly approved. If she remembered correctly, he had a metal stud through his tongue, and its abrasive feel had worked wonders on her clitoris.

'Hi. Remember me?' she said, flung open the driver's door and stuck out her long legs, giving him an eyeful. 'How about if I leave my car here? OK?'

'Sure,' he grunted, grinning widely. 'You're Kelly Cameron, right?'

'Right,' she said, and nodded to a van. 'I did some work on that when I was at Mike's garage.'

'I know. I was there. I fucked you legless in the storeroom.'

'So. I can say we're with you, if anyone asks?'

'Sure.'

'Thanks, Dave.'

'Any time, babe.'

The girls climbed out of the car. 'Now will you stop whinging?' Kelly said, and stood within Dave's sight, smoothing down her short leather skirt, fiddling with

22

the front lacing of her tight leather waistcoat, and adjusting the seams of her black stockings.

'He's getting a hard-on,' Caroline observed, as she looked in Tracy's wing mirror, taking out her lipstick and applying it to her wide mouth.

'I should hope so. I just might do something about that for him, later,' Kelly replied.

'He's cute, but is easy parking worth a blow-job?' Sally asked.

'You were the one who didn't want to walk.'

The other roadie strolled over. He had dreadlocks down to his waist and moved with lithe, Afro-Caribbean grace. His jeans fitted his arse to perfection, his chest rippled with muscle under a red vest, and his arms were like those of a prize-fighter. 'What's going on, man?' he asked Dave.

'Just some friends of mine. I've said they can park here.'

Caroline was looking at the black man speculatively. He was certainly impressive, handsome and smiling. 'I'm Caroline,' she said. 'And this is Sally, and Kelly. What's your name?'

'Grant,' he said, then dragged his gaze away from her and said to Dave, 'We'd better get moving. Alden's about to go into orbit.'

'Can you take us backstage?' Kelly asked, moving closer to Dave. 'I'd do just about anything to meet Alden.' She reached out and grasped his cock, hidden in those ball-crushingly tight Levi's.

He grunted and shot out an arm to pull her closer. She let go and backed off. He followed, and Grant grinned at him with a flash of gold-capped teeth and said, good-humouredly, 'You can't leave pussy alone, can you? Me, I'd rather keep Alden sweet. Plenty of time for that when the gig's over.'

Dave stuck his middle finger in the air in an abrasive gesture, then grasped Kelly's arm and said urgently, 'Don't take any notice of him. I want you now. Come on, let's do it. In the back of the van.'

Kelly weighed up the situation. It was true that she wanted an introduction to Alden Ray, the one all the girls raved about, but she wasn't really keen to pay for it by shagging Dave. I'm not that desperate, she thought, her agile mind running through the possibilities.

'Chill,' she said. 'Not now. Grant's right. And we don't want to rush things, do we? I feel like a long, leisurely seeing-to, not a quick shag in a smelly van that's been used for the gear. It stinks of fags, dope, beer and farts.'

Dave shrugged, and gave each of the women a light piece of equipment to carry. They entered the church by a side door which led to what had been the vestry, now refitted as dressing-rooms. A sound check was in progress on the stage. There were two support bands booked to play before the StingRayz. They started to come on to the girls.

Caroline and Sally weren't being picky, so Kelly put down the flight case and left them to it. She wandered off, searching for Alden, the tall, lean and tanned vocalist with the shaggy, bleached hair. Or possibly one of his four musicians, all of whom she liked.

The erstwhile nave was packed. Kelly nodded to various acquaintances, and moved on to a stall where StingRayz merchandise was on sale – T-shirts with the band's logo, mugs, badges and CDs. She was tempted to buy one, but hadn't enough money, so turned and scanned the notice board near the bar. There were flyers for art classes and writers' workshops, fire-breathing courses and lessons in how to become a shaman. The Centre was a haven for those with alternative views on religion, the meaning of life, the universe and everything. There was a definite leaning towards alternative medicine, and some of the brochures read like occult primers. Amongst the jostle of orange, shocking pink and blue printouts, there were several specialising in Tarot, palm or crystal readings.

Tucked away down one side, Kelly spotted a few cards advertising for employees. One was from a gift shop needing an assistant, another from a boutique, but a third caught her eye and pulled her up short. It was printed in Gothic lettering and read: 'The Falcon Bookshop needs a Girl or Boy Friday to help the proprietor look after the vast stock of books, old and new, prints and rare photographs in which we specialise'.

There was a phone number, an e-mail address and directions to the shop itself. Kelly recognised the name of the street, more of a lane really, crooked and cobbled, tucked away near the entrance to the Cathedral Close. She didn't have a pen and paper and knew she'd never memorise the number, so unpinned the card from the notice board and slipped it into her pocket.

Jobs for the girls, she thought, and that means Judith and me. They only ask for one helper, but I'll bet I can swing it so they take both of us. We'll ring tomorrow, or even go round there and suss it out.

The first band came on. They were average, and the crowd, except for a cluster of enthusiastic friends and relatives, didn't pay much heed. Kelly got herself a Coke, and made no attempt to elbow through to the front. She couldn't see Caroline or Sally. They were probably bonking the road crew somewhere.

By the time the second support group had finished, she was beginning to feel bored. There was an irritating pause, the air buzzing with impatience and pheromones as the StingRayz deliberately kept the fans waiting. A steady, hypnotic throb reverberated through the floor-standing speakers. It stirred up primitive, womb-state recollections of the maternal heartbeat.

Kelly used the opportunity to edge closer until she stood just below the proscenium.

The lights flashed and the drum-beat increased. Then the StingRayz exploded on to the stage in a flood of dry ice. Alden Ray dominated everything, his stance defiant and threatening as he staked out his territory. He was six feet two of raw sex. The crowd went wild as he belted out their favourite songs, then they quietened before erupting again as the band introduced unfamiliar material.

They played a stunning set, and it wasn't until after their fourth encore that they left the stage. By this time, Kelly was already out back, waiting for them, or rather, for Alden.

'Hello, Kelly,' Caroline called out, untangling her limbs from those of Chris, the road manager. He was balding, stocky and harassed-looking, and she had been sitting astride his lap, his fingers buried in her dark-fringed cunt.

'Jesus Christ! Are they done already? There's no rest for the wicked,' he exclaimed, wiping his wet hand down his shirt, tumbling Caroline from his knee and standing up. Hurriedly, he thrust his erection back in his trousers and zipped up his fly. 'Now they'll want to party, and I'm like a glorified nanny, keeping them out of trouble. They've been revamping the band, moving on to a "new evolution in music". Load of crap but it pleases the press. So they're in an even more crazy state than usual ... nerves, you see ... but the whole bloody lot are barking anyway, and I'm the poor bastard who has to wipe their arses and keep them out of nick.'

At that moment, Alden walked off the stage and snatched a beer from the waiting icebox.

Kelly stared, open-mouthed. He was still pumped-up with adrenalin, his sleeveless T-shirt clinging to his body, dark arcs of sweat under the armpits and at his back, his blond hair dripping.

Without speaking, he snapped open the tin and raised it to his lips. She watched, fascinated, as he drank, his Adam's apple bobbing up and down. His eyes were fixed on her the whole time. She had forgotten Caroline, Chris and the entire shebang. This was what she had come for – to have carnal knowledge of this creature who was sheer sex on legs.

'I'm going to shower, Chris,' he said casually. 'I'll talk to the press afterwards, OK?'

'OK,' Chris answered, and started to oversee the removal of equipment from the stage to the waiting vehicles.

'Come on,' Alden said to Kelly, and disappeared down a corridor.

Though piqued by such cavalier treatment, she couldn't resist following his order, lusting after his long legs and neat backside. More than this was the fire burning him up from inside – that enormous talent and ambition; she wanted a little of it to brush off on her.

She arrived at the dressing-room door. Alden was leaning against it, waiting for her. He let her through. It was deserted, though no doubt the rest of the group would be there soon. He crushed the can and lobbed it

27

into a rubbish bin. Then he stood spread-legged in front of the dressing-table mirror, unbuttoned his jeans, pulled them down over his thighs and took out his thick, meaty cock. Kelly stared at his reflection, so hot for him that her clit and labial wings were swollen, the thong of her black G-string wet with juice. The music and the sight of him gyrating his lean hips and controlling the audience in masterly fashion had been enough to turn her on completely.

'Do it,' he commanded, and she dropped to her knees in front of him, reaching up to pull him closer. She opened her mouth, unable to control herself.

He thrust towards her and she took his erection between her lips and sucked it in until it butted against the back of her throat, her face buried in his pubic hair. He was hot, sweaty and sexually aroused, his natural odour mingling with that of expensive body-spray. She plunged one hand into the gap between his thighs and grasped the heavy balls swinging there. She heard him sigh, and felt him start as she caressed them and ran a finger up his bottom, circling the tiny tight mouth of his anus.

His cock swelled even more, and she could taste jism and wondered if he would pull out or expect her to swallow his spunk. He grunted and reached down, touching her breast under the supple calfskin. Her nipples ached, rising to his touch, and she wanted to bare them for him. He withdrew from her mouth, seized her roughly round the waist and sat her on the dressing-table, scattering jars and make-up, cans and cigarette packets.

His fingers tangled with the lacing and she helped him, the two halves of the waistcoat falling open over her firm breasts, the nipples rising like cobnuts. He looked at them, then flicked them and she thrilled.

Those fingers had but lately wreaked havoc on his guitar strings, and now he was using them on her.

'Open your legs,' he said, fully hyped by the excitement and stress of performing live. It was this more than her that was making him so randy. Kelly was aware of this and trading on it, but didn't give a damn.

She let her thighs slide apart, and Alden stared down at her furry mons, bridged by the lycra triangle of her tanga. He tugged at it. It broke and fell away. He fingered her labial groove, wetted her clit with her copious dew and massaged it steadily. Screaming and clinging to him, Kelly came. She heard the rustle of a condom packet, then he pushed her back so that the mirror supported her. He lifted her hips and she felt his latex-covered prong hovering at her entrance, then the mighty force as he propelled it in with a swift heave of his agile pelvis. It was almost too much, and she angled herself to take him.

She looked into his face, imprinting it on her memory. When she was an old, old lady she would remember that Alden Ray had once fucked her. It was better than having him sign an autograph book. He wore that absorbed expression which possessed him when he was playing, a kind of communion with an unseen world. What did he see behind those closed eyelids? Was it her? Or was he lost in the realms of music? It was more likely that, like any other bloke, he was thinking of nothing but ridding his balls of semen, she thought cynically.

She locked her legs round his hips, picturing how lewd she must look with those black-seamed stockings clipped to gilt suspenders, her strappy shoes crossed at the ankles, the stilt heels digging into Alden's bum, and her wet, eager pussy plugged by his engorged cock. In a sudden fit of abandonment, she wished the room would fill with people – his fans, his groupies, the news-hounds, the other musicians. She wanted to display herself to the world, her private parts becoming very public indeed.

He was pumping faster, and she put her hand down and rotated her thumb on her clitoris. She wanted to climax again. One orgasm was never enough for her. She could feel it mounting, the friction on her bud and the exact point inside her vagina sensitive to his probing penis, all combining to bring on her crisis.

'Yes! Yes!' she screeched, and was swept to the peak, then tumbled down as she felt his cock twitch and the heat increase inside her as he discharged his load into the condom.

He leaned against her and his breathing slowed. There was a commotion at the door and the rest of the band charged in, waving lager bottles and hallooing. They stopped, wolf-whistled, and shouted with glee when they saw their singer with his dick still buried in Kelly's quim.

'Hey, Ald! Got any spare? Can we have a go?' they chorused.

He withdrew from her. 'Wow! What a stonker! The last time I saw anything like that was at a stud farm,' observed the drummer.

Alden ignored them and rolled off the condom. The teat was full of creamy emission. He tossed it into the bin.

Kelly abandoned her torn panties and stood up, adjusting her clothing. The group were sitting around discussing the next show. She was ready to go, and Alden looked up and said, 'I'd ask you to stay, but we're not putting up in a hotel tonight. We're leaving right away and kipping in the bus. Got to get up north for tomorrow night's gig.'

'That's cool. You'll be able to add this to those apocryphal tales of life on tour,' she said pleasantly, but with a touch of acid. 'I got what I came for. Goodbye.' And she leaned over and casually brushed his cheek with her lips.

He looked surprised, but said nothing. Kelly let herself out of the room.

She couldn't find Sally or Caroline, and decided to go home. They could always take a taxi when they'd had enough of screwing strangers. She glanced at her watch. It was long past midnight. Sitting in Tracy's driving seat, she came across the business card in her waistcoat pocket. She scanned it in the dashboard light. Tomorrow she'd do something about it. She'd had enough of playing around. Time to get her life into some sort of order.

'Sure, I had a great time. I was shagged bandy by Alden Ray,' Kelly said to Judith over breakfast next morning. Then she laid a printed card on the table between the low-fat spread and the marmalade and added, 'What d'you think about this? We should both apply.'

Judith picked it up and studied it thoughtfully. 'Looks interesting.'

'Doesn't it just? You phone while I get ready. See if we can go today.'

Judith wished Kelly would do it, though she knew she couldn't put off job-hunting indefinitely. It was the thought of offering her services and being rejected that scared her. She was already dressed, having got up early. Peter had gone home around eleven last night. He could have stayed but, though he didn't say, she guessed his mother would have given him a hard time. I may be free, she concluded, but he certainly

31

isn't. She experienced again the impatience that had surged through her as he kissed her goodnight at the front door. Didn't he want to experience the feeling of sleeping beside her and taking her in his arms when they woke? He really was a tepid lover.

She picked up the cordless phone and pressed a sequence of numbers. It started to ring at the other end. She almost replaced the instrument, then a voice said, 'The Falcon Bookshop. May I help you?'

It was a male voice, deep, cultured and oddly seductive. Judith gulped, and replied, 'I saw your advertisement for an assistant . . . at least my friend did. We'd both like to come along for an interview.'

There was a pause.

'How about after lunch? Shall we make it two o'clock?' he said, and she detected a hint of amusement in his voice. 'Who shall I expect?'

'Oh, ah . . . I'm Judith Shaw and my friend is Kelly Cameron.'

'My name is Adam Renald and I own the bookshop. I look forward to meeting you this afternoon, Miss Shaw.'

'Oh . . . yes. Thank you,' she stammered. She had a strange feeling that he was waiting for her to say more, but then he rang off.

Tracy was left in the municipal parking lot outside the town hall, and Judith and Kelly walked through the narrow streets in search of their quarry. It wasn't hard to find. The shop had bow windows with dimpled glass, white paintwork and an oak door. Spring bulbs were sending up green spears in the square wooden planters on each side. There were books and old maps on display behind the small-paned casements, and a bell tinkled as they pushed open the door and walked in.

Only the portentous ticking of a grandfather clock broke the silence. They stood there for a moment, then Kelly called out, 'Shop!' There was no reply, so she said to Judith, 'That's weird. Let's take a look around.'

'Maybe we shouldn't. Perhaps I got it wrong,' Judith suggested.

'Don't be daft. There's bound to be someone here. They wouldn't leave the place unlocked.'

Kelly was always so practical, forthright and outspoken. She never lost her nerve and Judith envied her. Chameleon-like, she was able to adapt to different places and situations. This afternoon, she had left behind her casual clothes and was wearing a smart, tailored suit in dark grey flannel. It emphasised her long legs and neat waist, and didn't disguise the fullness of her breasts. A fiery orange silk blouse added a dramatic note, and she had tamed her wayward hair, trapping it in a black velvet scrunchie.

Kelly also carried a file containing her CV, and Judith knew this to be equally impressive. True, she'd worked with cars and was a first-class mechanic, but this had only been a hobby. In reality she was highly qualified and had left university with a degree in computer science. Fond as she was of her friend, Judith was sometimes gnawed by an ignoble emotion. Jealousy and envy were ugly things, but it didn't seem fair that Kelly should be so glamorous and clever into the bargain.

Now she was wandering round the shop, completely at ease, while Judith was uncertain. She caught a glimpse of herself in an antique mirror and, though she had made an effort and been pleased with the result, she now decided that she looked as dowdy as ever. Her confidence sank.

The shop was an Aladdin's Cave of treasures.

33

Shelves lined the walls, each filled with books, both new and second-hand. There were others behind glass doors, heavy tomes with leather covers and gilt lettering on their spines. A globe rotated on its ebony stand, and Judith judged this to be no reproduction, but a genuine Victorian piece. There were prints and maps and works of art, and a few, very select ornaments: Chinese figurines in jade in a locked cabinet, other oriental trinkets of great value, and telescopes, binoculars and cameras from a bygone age.

But books dominated the shop, occupying every spare corner, table surface and stand. They gave off a distinctive smell, of libraries in stately homes and printers' ink.

Judith was seized by a burning desire to work there. She could feel herself breathing in the erudite atmosphere, dizzy with the wealth of knowledge that would be available should Mr Renald decide to take her on. She wanted the job with a passion that knew no bounds.

'Oh, Kelly, it's wonderful! What a place!' she exclaimed, her enthusiasm drowning out any misgivings she might have had.

'It's OK,' Kelly answered. 'I think we can manage this very well between us. But where's our mysterious interviewer?'

Judith suddenly stopped, her head tilted at an angle, a frown drawing her brows together. She had the unnerving feeling that they were being watched. Icy fingers trailed down her spine and she felt an urge to run. She didn't mention this to Kelly, afraid that she'd make fun of her, but her delight at the prospect of being an assistant took a nose-dive.

'Ah, there you are,' said a voice, and a man materialised from behind a velvet curtain. 'I'm sorry to have kept you. Miss Shaw and Miss Cameron, I presume. I'm Adam Renald.'

Judith was rooted to the spot. Not only had he startled her, but his very presence took her breath away. He was in his mid-thirties, a spare, sinewy man wearing jeans and a sweatshirt that bore the words *The Falcon Bookshop* and the design of a hawk. He looked studious, with rumpled brown hair, worn rather long and curling round his neck, and a thin, handsome face with a strong nose. A pair of reading glasses were pushed high on his forehead.

She could see that Kelly was taking in every inch of him, as she always did when introduced to a new man. Judith imagined what she would say about him later. Would she give him ten out of ten for a neat backside?

'Kelly Cameron. Nice to meet you,' Kelly said, and held out her hand in a businesslike manner.

He took it, shook it and let it drop, saying, 'The pleasure is mine.' He turned to Judith and added, 'So you must be Miss Shaw?'

'That's correct. Judith Shaw.'

'Ah, and it was you who rang me. I recognise your voice. Well, now, come into the office. Would you like some coffee, or tea, perhaps? Don't worry about security. There are cameras and a screen. I can see everything that goes on in the shop.'

'So you saw us?' Judith said brightly.

'Oh, yes. I saw you,' he answered coolly.

He was an attentive host and a beguiling prospective boss. 'I've had several applicants already,' he said, when seated at his old-fashioned roll-top desk, pivoting in the leather upholstered office chair, circa 1900. 'But I can't find one person who possesses the skills I require.'

'Maybe you're expecting too much. Two people

35

might be better,' Kelly suggested, crossing her trousered legs at the knee and holding her coffee cup with all the aplomb of a duchess.

Again, Judith admired her style. She had adapted seamlessly to the aura of old-world charm that surrounded both Adam and his shop. Gone was the loud swinger who went clubbing; the feisty, up-tight feminist with attitude; the tough cookie who pulled blokes then left them high if not dry. No longer using street-speak, she had taken on an upper-class accent, similar to his.

'You may be right,' Adam agreed. He glanced through her CV and one of his eyebrows lifted. 'Very impressive, Miss Cameron,' he observed.

'Oh, please. No formality. Call me Kelly,' she said, meeting his gaze frankly, a smile curving her sensual lips.

'I need someone who is computer literate,' he went on, though his eyes lingered, leaving her face and drifting downwards to her breasts. 'I want to set up a website listing the contents of my shop, offering books and other items for sale on the Internet.'

'A piece of cake,' Kelly responded airily.

'And then there's the question of somebody to serve the customers, answer the phone, that sort of thing. Do you feel capable of taking this on, Miss Shaw?'

Judith had to pull herself together and concentrate. She had been meandering in a dream in which she and Adam were cruising the River Isis at Oxford, she in a georgette dress, à la Roaring Twenties, and Adam wearing white flannels, striped blazer and straw boater as he poled the punt along.

'I beg your pardon. Say again,' she faltered, feeling the blood rise to her cheeks.

'Would you like to work here, serving in the shop?'

he repeated, and, seeing him exchange a glance with Kelly, she wished the floor would open and swallow her up.

'Yes. I'd like that very much,' she mumbled, then lifted her chin stubbornly and added, 'If you look at my CV, you'll see that I majored in history and literature, and didn't do too badly in languages either. I can speak French, German and Italian.'

Her voice gained strength as she went on, remembering Kelly's advice about not hiding her light under a bushel. Having got over her earlier fright, realising that it must have been Adam who was watching them through the monitor, she was even more determined not to leave without him making her an offer.

He gave a faint smile, and casually got to his feet. 'Perhaps you'd both like to see some of the material I'll need you to handle,' he said, and stepped towards a door at the back.

It creaked open and he switched on a naked light-bulb. Judith found herself walking through a maze of shelves, each crowded with books, and then into a white-walled room where he drew out large, shallow drawers containing prints. Leaning over his shoulder, Judith could not restrain a gasp. Old, they certainly were – seventeenth- and eighteenth-century originals, no doubt – but their contents were explicit in the extreme. The blush that had never quite left her face since meeting Adam now deepened.

Kelly, however, chuckled and said, 'Wow! And who said sex was invented for the delectation and delight of today's younger generation?'

'Who, indeed?' Adam said, regarding her with a smile. His eyes slid back to Judith and she knew he was waiting for her to make a comment.

'Interesting,' was all she could manage.

37

To her horror she realised that she was becoming aroused. Adam was standing very close to her, and she wanted to stretch out her hand and caress his lean, smooth-shaven jaw. How would it feel if she went lower, trailing her fingers across his broad chest, tracing the printed hawk and going down further? Would he stop her? Or would he accept her homage as she followed the outline of his penis that hung against his left thigh under the blue jeans?

Her breathing was shallow, her nipples uncomfortably hard beneath the restricting sports bra. It was so plain and functional that she would have been embarrassed if he'd seen it. A picture of aubergine, claret and black brassières floated in her fevered imagination. Lace-trimmed wired cups that would lift her breasts, baring her teats. Or, even more daring, bras with open tips so that her nipples poked through, tempting as wild strawberries. As for her knickers? It was just as well they were so substantial and able to soak up her juices. She had never been so wet, not even when daydreaming of Marcus.

She yearned for split-crotch panties in garish colours that matched the visionary bras. She wanted to wear tarty suspenders and fishnet stockings, and flaunt herself on high, high heels. She was sick of dressing modestly and being demure and ultra good.

The prints inspired her as Adam turned them over, page by page. Black and white lithographs of the school of Rawlings or Hogarth, reproduced on sturdy paper. They depicted big-busted whores and raffish gentlemen with their cocks poking out of their breeches; women sprawling on couches, laughing, abandoned, while men fingered their hairy cunts and naked dugs. Young men peeped from behind curtains while lesbians made love. Priests, cassocks lifted, handled their balls, while blushing maidens knelt before them in a strange act of worship, slurping at their enlarged organs.

'But my real interest lies in photography,' Adam said, closing the drawers containing prints and sliding out others. From these he lifted heavy, leather-bound albums, made in the last century or earlier. He raised the cover of one, displaying a set of faded brownish pictures. They were photographs of models posing as if caught in the heat of passion. The equipment of the time dictated that they remain still. Even so, the voluptuous bodies of the women, their languorous eyes staring straight at the camera, while their mustachioed lovers advanced erect cocks towards their cracks, offered a naughty, forbidden thrill.

'They're pornographic,' Kelly said, inching forward to take a closer look.

'Yes, and these are but a few I have for sale. They are very valuable,' Adam explained, and Judith could hardly look at him, certain he would somehow read the thoughts whirling inside her head and be aware of the needy ache in her groin. 'I want you to catalogue most things here, Kelly, though not these or the lithographs,' he went on. 'I don't want information about them going out on the network. In this sensitive field, I deal with private buyers on a personal level. Do you understand?'

'Does this mean you are offering me the job as your computer person?' Kelly asked.

'Yes. We'll discuss terms, of course, and there will be a contract,' he said, putting the photographs away and locking the drawers.

'How much?' she demanded.

'That's negotiable.'

'I'll give it my best shot. And Judith?'

'Of course, if that's agreeable to her. Is it, Judith?' And he turned his head and fixed her with his steel-grey eyes. She couldn't look away, drawn like a needle to a magnet.

'Yes. Thank you. Oh, yes! That will be fine,' she stammered, clasping her hands to her breasts, unable to think of anything other than: He's taking me on. He thinks I can do it.

He touched her arm and a frisson of excitement shot down to her clit. 'Good. We'll talk about the money and hours of employment in a while. I suggest we have another coffee and toast our new relationship.'

'As boss and employees?' Kelly put in sharply.

'Something like that,' he said smoothly, and took them back to the office. 'When can you start?'

Kelly exchanged a glance with Judith, then said, 'Tomorrow, if you like.'

'I do like. Tomorrow it is.'

'Those rude photos and drawings? Wild! To say nothing of him and his shop.' Kelly couldn't wait to chew the interview over with Judith, linking an arm with hers as they sauntered back to the car. 'Is he a dish or what? Who's going to fuck him first, you or me?'

'I don't want ... I shan't ... oh, Kelly!' Judith gasped, blushing furiously.

'Don't have a coronary. I'm kidding.' But this was a lie, and Kelly was already speculating on how easy it would be to seduce Adam Renald.

He had offered them a salary that was higher than either had expected. They'd work the obligatory month before getting the first wage packet, but Kelly reckoned they could just about survive until then.

Presumably, this would be a trial period, but she had no doubt that he'd want to continue employing them, especially if they threw in a few unexpected sexy treats.

'Let's have fish and chips for tea to celebrate,' she carolled, as Tracy purred into life.

'All right, but I want you to know, Kelly, that I haven't any designs on Mr Renald. I'm glad to have a job and I know I'm going to enjoy it,' Judith said primly, staring straight ahead as they drove towards the motorway.

'And there's Peter, of course,' Kelly retorted, irritated by such piety, which she was convinced masked a libido eager and ready to expand and enjoy itself.

'Yes. He's my boyfriend, after all. I owe him my loyalty.'

'You owe him sweet FA. Isn't he a wrist-slashingly boring fuck?'

'Well . . .'

'Stop it, Judith. You've grown out of him. Get a life.'

'You think I should dump him? Try someone else?'

'Way to go,' Kelly said. 'I'm going to do a makeover on you, my girl. Under that façade there's a ravishingly beautiful nymphet trying to get out.'

At five-thirty, Adam locked the shop door, turned the sign so that it read CLOSED, and let himself into the passage that connected the shop to his flat. He mounted the single flight of stairs and entered the upper hall and then the living room.

The arrangement suited him well – the shop, the large apartment above it, the balcony at the rear with steps leading into a secluded garden. There was even a double garage reached from a side road. Adam had bought the property several years before and hadn't

41

once regretted his investment. He was a bachelor and glad of it. There was never a shortage of sexual relief in his life and he wasn't doomed to celibacy – far from it.

He picked up the phone and punched in the number. He heard it ringing at its destination, but she didn't answer right away. She wouldn't, of course. She'd guess it was him but choose to keep him on tenterhooks. He could see her in his mind's eye, that flaxen-haired woman with the glorious figure and inspiring legs, who owned him body and soul.

'Yes? Who is it?' he heard her say at last, and the hairs stood up at the back of his neck as his body responded to her husky voice.

'It's me, Adam,' he answered.

'How did it go?' she said, and he thought he heard a faint rustle, as if she was stretching out on the deeply cushioned couch in her boudoir.

'What are you wearing?' he whispered, with a catch in his breath.

'I asked you a question,' she returned, cuttingly. 'But if you must know, I'm dressed in a long skirt that opens all the way down the front, and a strapless bodice.'

'Tell me more. Talk to me about your underclothes,' he begged. He could feel his cock rising, rock-hard, within his trousers.

'Not yet. The young women. Did you interview them?'

Adam was in torment. He balanced the phone between his shoulder and his chin and unfastened his flies. His cock jutted out, easily finding its way to freedom. It had been chafing in there all the time he was with Kelly and Judith.

'I saw them, Anna,' he said, closing his fist round his erection and working it up and down.

'And?'

42

'They are perfect. I've offered them both a job. They start tomorrow. Kelly is sharp, bright and worldly, but Judith is just what you're looking for, I believe – naïve and vulnerable. Plainer than Kelly, but she needs bringing out of herself to reach her full potential.'

'Good. I shall tell Damian. You've done well,' Anna purred.

'All I want is to please you,' he began.

'Haven't you forgotten something?' she hissed sharply.

'Oh, yes. Forgive me . . . *mistress*.'

'That's better. Are you wanking, Adam?'

'Yes, mistress.'

'Tell me what you're feeling.'

Adam was finding it difficult to concentrate, every nerve, sinew and blood cell gathering force to make him discharge his libation. Without the smallest hesitation he wanted to offer this as a tribute to Anna. She was his goddess, his adored one. His queen.

'I can't, at this minute. I want to come so badly.'

'Talk to me! Do it. If you disobey, you know you'll be punished next time we meet.'

The thought drove through his loins like a forest fire. His buttocks burned and old bruises throbbed. Anna was a wonder with the whip. She knew there was a fine line between agony and excruciating pleasure.

'I'm thinking of you, mistress,' he gasped, his fingers flying over his rigid stem, the dew pooling in his helm's single eye. 'I imagine your beautiful breasts, and want to play with those marvellous nipples. I see your cunt, swept clean of hair and glistening, the diamonds in your clitoris ring sparkling against your sun-kissed skin.'

'Go on,' she commanded throatily. 'What am I doing, slave?'

43

He hazarded a guess. 'Toying with your bud? Rubbing your slit and wetting it, then circling the pink pearl that crowns it.'

'Very good,' she murmured, and he could hear the slurp, slurp of a finger on wet labial flesh as she held the earpiece of the phone to her pussy.

'Jesus Christ!' Adam groaned, jism oozing into his palm, the tension in his balls rising, spreading, flooding his spine with fire.

'You're not to come until I say you can,' Anna ordered, but her voice was no longer firm and he knew she was about to reach crisis point.

'Pretty pussy,' he whispered to hurry her along, needing to chase his own climax. 'Kelly and Judith will be your playthings. Their breasts, their cunts, their mouths, all ready to be serviced by you and to pleasure you in return.'

'Ah . . . ah . . . yes! I'm there. Oh, God!'

He listened to her screaming and knew she'd come. He bent his knees slightly, thrust his pelvis up and rubbed his prick furiously. Now it was beyond his control. As he listened to Anna sighing at the other end of the line, his milky spunk shot from him – once, twice, three times. His hand was covered in it. His knees were shaking and he collapsed into a chair. His cock was shrinking, though still engorged, and he caressed it soothingly, wishing his new assistants were present. He'd soon teach them to assist him in other ways than on the computer and in the shop.

As if reading his mind, Anna, fully recovered and brisk, said, 'Arrange for Damian and me to meet Kelly and Judith. I want to start training them right away.'

'Yes, mistress,' Adam said, and put down the phone.

Chapter 3

A THOUGHTFUL SMILE PLAYED around Anna Cresswell's full, poppy-red lips as she reflected on the conversation with her slave, agent and procurer. Adam was more than just useful in tracking down antiquities. He shared her enthusiasm for the 'scene', ever willing to find new recruits. She held the phone in the tips of her manicured fingers, then replaced the receiver.

The room was darkening and she reached out to click on the table lamp. A glow irradiated the apricot silk shade. It added to the warmth of the décor, feminine and earthy, harking back to Art Nouveau, each item handpicked for its sinuously graceful design. She and Damian were connoisseurs when it came to antiques, but extended their extraordinary recognition of all things rare and beautiful to the living human form.

And what better place in which to display their finds than the Rectory? They had bought this gracious old house two years before, needing a refuge from London, a bolthole where they could retire when the pace got too hot. It was a rabbit warren of a place, and had cost them a fortune to restore, but was well worth every penny. Anna glanced round her boudoir, with its Chinese wallpaper and white skirtings, the ceiling ornamented with plaster roses and acanthus leaves, the carpets Persian, the furniture in keeping with the Rectory's date of construction in the last quarter of the nineteenth century. It was luxurious, and would have been approved by the rectors who had lived there in the past. More often than not these had been used to living well, possibly the second sons of wealthy families who had been earmarked for the church, but they might have looked askance at the activities that now took place beneath its roof.

She smiled again as she thought of the cellars, transformed into sadomasochistic dungeons where friends might indulge their whims. Perhaps those sober-sided gentlemen might have been interested after all. No doubt they did their fair share of chastisement when it came to lazy servants and recalcitrant offspring, even taking the rod to erring wives. Dirty buggers, she concluded, amused yet mildly irritated by the hypocrisy rife in those days. There was a vast amount of evidence pointing to the secret life of the well-to-do Victorians; God-fearing on the surface, but avid consumers of the pornography available, covering their tracks by declaring an interest in science and art.

Males only, of course, Anna thought. The ladies were not allowed to look. Their men staunchly protected them, announcing that if such material was viewed by children, the working classes or *women*, they would be corrupted, their base instincts aroused – nay, *animal instincts*, as they were so much closer to the beasts than gentlemen.

Anna shivered as she visualised a forceful husband who looked like Jane Eyre's Mr Rochester, lifting her crinoline, pulling down her drawers and whacking her bare bottom because he had caught her tampering with his library. Oh boy, she thought. What a turn on!

'Who was that on the phone?' A masculine voice pulled her sharply to attention and, as she looked across at its owner, a pang of lust and longing shot through her.

Not Mr Rochester, but pretty damn close.

Damian Cresswell was an exceedingly striking man, even when, as now, he was barefoot from the shower, a towel looped round his narrow hips, another wound turban-like about his handsome head. His features were chiselled and masculine, with high cheekbones, a sensually cruel mouth and sherry-coloured, heavy-lidded eyes. He had inherited his pronounced good looks from his mother, Magda, who had been a French aristocrat, impoverished and down on her luck until she had come to England, then met and married Sir Roderick Cresswell, landowner and peer. The result of this odd union, for Roderick had been thirty years her senior, was their only child, Damian.

When the old man died, trouble had ensued. He had an heir by his former wife, and this man had inherited the family estate and everything in it, though he couldn't deny Damian the substantial sum bequeathed to him by a doting father. Magda had felt herself slighted and made a tremendous fuss, involving lawyers, court hearings and other tedious nonsense that had cost her dear, achieved nothing, and eventually brought on a fatal heart-attack.

'That, my darling, was Adam,' Anna replied, arousal grabbing at her loins. The incident with the bookseller had left her craving another orgasm. Now she wanted more than a finger-fuck. She wanted a full-on encounter with Damian, where she could revel in his domination and his wonderfully large cock.

She had never seen one like it, and her experience of male equipment was legion, from the time she was a teenage convent-school pupil, through episodes in country houses and at 'coming out' balls, a stint as a stripper – not by necessity, just for the hell of it – and bit parts in porn movies. Anna had been born with a silver spoon in her mouth. On maturing she had quickly exchanged this for flesh, finding her forte as a high-class hooker and dominatrix.

And when she had finally caught up with her cousin Damian, who already had a formidable reputation as an art dealer and hedonist, he had completed her sexual education. He became her master, mentor and lover. They complemented one another superbly: stunningly attractive, talented and clever. Party-animals, though not in the conventional sense. In each of them, possibly inherited from some mutual rogue gene, was the need to experiment. They pushed the boundaries, exploring to the limits the dichotomy of pain and pleasure. They were powerful personalities who liked to be in control.

'And what did he have to say?' Damian asked as he strolled across, placed a hand on each of her knees and prised them apart. His eyes narrowed like a stalking tiger's, and he inhaled deeply, adding softly, 'I can smell your cunt. You've just come, haven't you? Was it while you were talking to him? My dear, you torture that man.'

'And he loves it,' she murmured, then gasped as his strong fingers palpated her clitoris, the hood retracting over the jewel that pierced it.

'I shall have to chastise you,' he said firmly, then freed his tousled, blue-black hair, sat on the daybed close to the window embrasure and ordered her to 'Come here.'

Anna gulped, her heart beating quickly, her inner self becoming lubricious. Her eyes were glued to his punishment hand. He moved fast. Within a split second she was over a pair of muscular thighs. His towel had fallen off and she could see his semi-erect phallus lifting towards her side, and the shape of his balls resting between his legs on the upholstered seat. He smelled strongly of shower gel, aftershave and genitalia. She was excited by his personal body odour, and sometimes tested herself to prove that she would recognise it among many others, in the same way that she'd know his cock blindfold, by its shape, circumference and the way it curved a little to the right.

'Oh, master! Don't hurt me! I'm sorry if I've offended you,' she cried, acting out her submissive role.

'You *will* be sorry by the time I've finished with you,' he growled, and his cock grew another inch, rearing upwards against his hairy belly. 'Now, slave, tell me precisely what Adam said. No lies or bending the truth, or you'll suffer for it. I shall use the rod, not my hand, and you'll merit twelve strokes.'

She shivered when he used that harsh, merciless tone, and said, 'He has taken on fresh members of staff. Two young women, one confident and the other shy. He says they are perfect for us.'

'And we shall see them soon?'

'Very soon, master. He will devise a plan.'

'Oh? He will not. He'll do as I tell him, and so will you, disgusting little bitch-slave!'

She lay across his lap, her stomach and ribs supported by his rock-hard thighs, her straight pale hair tumbling down almost to the floor. His ribs and chest were muscle-packed. He practised martial arts and fencing, training with his teachers, one Japanese, the other an Olympic medallist who had won gold for épée and sabre. No matter how she squirmed and fought, he would always conquer. There were times when he chose to enter into combat with her, liking to have her pit herself against his strength, but not today.

She didn't attempt to struggle. She was his sub, his slave, in fetish parlance the 'bottom', while he was the 'top'. And, as she stayed still while he pushed up her black velvet bodice and exposed her breasts, she knew a confusion of desire, aching need and anticipation. He unfastened her wrap-around skirt, and it slithered to the ground. She wore no panties, and her naked arse rose into view, two flawless mounds of bronzed skin. Like him, she strove for a seamless, all-year tan, jet-setting round the world in pursuit of the sun.

His hands massaged her rump, and she spread her legs, wanting to feel his fingers in her hole, using the motion of coitus, then moving higher, entering forbidden territory, easing the way for his penetration of her rectum. His touch was so soothing, and the few slaps he administered aroused her even more. She squirmed, lifted her hips towards him, inviting further invasion.

'Please, master. Make me come,' she pleaded.

He slapped her harder, a stinging blow. 'I'll do what I want to do, when I'm ready. You have no say in the matter, slave.'

'No, master,' she whimpered.

His blows fell like driving rain then, and the heat in her backside intensified. She was sure it must be bright red. At brief intervals, he stopped to lay his palm on her skin, his other hand tweaking her nipples and rolling them into hard, needy peaks.

'I shall enjoy indoctrinating Adam's young ladies,'

he mused, and his cock twitched, its bare, purplish head dribbling dew.

'And may I enjoy them, too?' she asked, wriggling her breasts into his palm.

'I shall give you orders. If they're novices, they will need shaving, piercing, and stretching. You'll insert butt-plugs. They shall be restrained and subdued. Oh, yes, Anna, there will be much for you to do.'

'Thank you, master,' she murmured.

Once again he brought her to the threshold of unbearable pain, then backed off and rubbed her bud. She wanted to scream for more. The intense burning in her buttocks communicated with her clit, and she tried to reach down and rub it, but he slapped her hand away, barking, 'No. I'll decide when you come. I may not let you. Perhaps I'll make you wear a chastity belt so you can't masturbate.'

This was a horrendous punishment and one that she had sometimes endured for days on end. It was humiliating, too, for Damian kept the key of this metal, cup-shaped object that covered her pubis, strapped close with chains circling her waist. Whenever she needed to relieve herself, she was forced to ask him to unlock it.

There were moments when she hated him, yet she couldn't argue now when he said, 'I'm doing you a favour, Anna. See how concerned I am about your welfare. You're a dirty slut, who'd be running riot, screwing everything that breathed, if I didn't stop you. Isn't that the truth?'

He smacked her so hard that she bucked, trying unsuccessfully to rub her mound against his thigh. 'Yes, yes, master. You know best,' she agreed, hoping that he'd soon get tired of the game and either frig her to completion or stick his cock in her.

'I do,' he said, and walloped her meanly, until tears ran down her cheeks and dripped to the floor. 'Just remember that, bitch.'

He spanked her six more times, then tumbled her from his lap. She landed awkwardly, in a heap at his feet. He rose from the daybed and grabbed her, then pushed her down on to it. The seat was still warm from him, and its heat joined that of the scalding pain in her bottom.

'Open them,' he shouted, and she spread her legs.

He took one of the thick, heavily fringed cords that held back the window drapes and tied her arms behind her. She was used to this kind of treatment, welcoming it, looking at his naked prick swollen to great size, and feeling that hot, heavy sensation in her pussy at the thought of being penetrated by that meaty spear.

He stood above her, lifted his hips and brought his cock to her mouth. 'Suck it,' he commanded.

She opened her mouth and rubbed her lips over its sticky helm. Her tongue ran lightly round the ridge where his foreskin would have rolled back, had he not been circumcised. She could never make up her mind whether she preferred a man cut or au naturel. His glans looked huge, shiny and red, seeping clear drops of lubrication that were sweet to her taste buds. She teased and played with it, until he dragged her forward, his hands in her hair, holding her firmly to his weapon.

She could feel his nails abrading her scalp, his need so great that he was in danger of losing his much-prided control. Who was the dominator and who the slave now? she wondered. She sucked hard, her mouth so tight that her cheeks caved in. He groaned and clenched his teeth. She thought he was going to lose it, but he held on. Pulling back, he sat down and spread her over his knees again, her hands still bound. He smacked her, then rubbed her furiously. She wanted the pain, needed the shame, her body on fire.

He alternated between slaps and dropping his hand to her clit. Her desire mounted, pain and desire intermingled, and she came in a rush. Then he rolled her over, parted her legs and rammed his cock into her, taking her with greedy, ruthless intensity. Her vagina contracted round him and, as he exploded, she tightened her internal grip.

He withdrew and eased her bonds away. She lay there with her eyes closed. He was right: a woman like her needed a man who would do brutal things to her.

She was tired, her thinking muddled. Her backside felt scorched. It radiated warmth to the rest of her body. Damian left her, reached for the towel and wiped himself, the condom discarded. She hadn't been aware of him putting one on, but guessed she had been too preoccupied.

'This is what we'll teach our new pupils, eh?' he said, smiling down at her, the shape of his lips, the sight of his mouth making her want to kiss him and lose herself in him again.

'Oh, yes,' she replied languidly, as he brought over drinks and sat beside her, fondling her gently until she purred. 'I almost envy them. They're about to enter our world and learn our wicked ways.'

'What on earth shall I wear? I've nothing suitable,' Judith wailed, going through her clothes for the umpteenth time.

'What are you like? You'll do just great. He fancied you as you were today, remember? A wholesome, homespun gal,' Kelly answered, curled up on Judith's bed, adding another coat of blue lacquer to her toenails. She had cotton wool stuffed between each one and was wearing a bathrobe, preparing herself in her own way.

'I'm certain I'll never sleep a wink.'

'You will. If in doubt, get Peter round. I find a snog relaxes me. Oh, I forgot, he's not gifted at that, is he? More likely to wind you up even more. I'll bet Adam knows his way around.'

'I don't want to think about that,' Judith said, thoroughly agitated. She yanked a cerise flared skirt and matching loose jacket from the cupboard and held them against her, staring woefully in the mirror. 'What d'you think?'

'No,' Kelly said decisively. 'They don't do a thing for you. Where on earth did you find them? In a charity shop?'

'No. Charity shops usually come up with goodies. Mrs Tanner advised me to buy them when I went to a clothing party with her. One of her friends was running it. I weakened and it took me ages to pay for them on the never-never. I've haven't even worn them.'

'I'm not surprised, they're dowdy in the extreme. I wouldn't be seen dead in them. Get rid. The dustbin or Oxfam – anything, but just stop contaminating the cottage.'

Judith folded the offending garments and placed them in a black plastic bin-liner which was filling rapidly. She was thoroughly dissatisfied with her wardrobe, but was confused, having not yet discovered her own, individual way of dressing.

'Don't sling that,' Kelly said suddenly as a denim skirt was about to follow the rest, destined to help the aged or buy rice for famine victims.

'No? But it doesn't suit me. I'm not a denim kind of person,' Judith protested, though admitting to herself that she had hoped this impulse buy might make her feel sporty and carefree. It hadn't, and Peter had expressed a dislike of the fabric, loops, hip pockets, brass buttons and all.

'It's common,' he had stated firmly. 'I hope I never see you in jeans, Judith.'

'You wear them,' she had pointed out feebly.

'That's got nothing to do with it.'

How could she argue with that? She'd shoved the skirt to the back of her hanging rail, hidden by others, and hadn't thought about it again until now.

'That's crap. Denim suits everyone,' Kelly stated, stretching out her legs and admiring her blue nails. 'And it's in again. The street look. The sort of thing your mother would hate. That skirt's stonewashed, and a tad out of date, but pop it on.'

Judith did as she was told. It was short and fitted her hips like a second skin. Ineffectually, she tugged at the hem, but it still rested stubbornly halfway between her knees and her upper thighs.

'I'll have to be careful or my knickers will show,' Judith said, marvelling at how much longer her legs looked, though she thought them gawky and coltish.

'That's the idea, isn't it?' Kelly grinned mischievously.

'Not mine,' Judith answered. To her horror, she thought of tomorrow morning, of arriving for her first day at work wearing the skirt. Would Adam try for a glimpse of her panties?

'Why not? You've got a wicked pair of legs. And those thick black stockings and white suspenders make you look wild, sort of St Trinian's naughty girl, birching and hot bottoms, and lesbian romps in the dorm.' Kelly bounced on the bed, hooting with laughter.

'I don't think so,' Judith said, and went to take it off.

'No, don't,' Kelly commanded. 'We've got to find a T-shirt to go with it. Wait here.'

She dashed off to her room and returned smartly, carrying several possibilities. She held out a white one. It was short and tight and had the words *Eve was Framed* printed across the chest.

Reluctantly, Judith discarded her blouse and pulled the T-shirt over her head. It really was short, baring her midriff. 'I shall be too cold,' she complained, regarding herself in the mirror.

She looked different, the mini-skirt and brief top with its feminist logo bringing about a transformation she wasn't sure she liked. Kelly seemed delighted, hovering around her busily. In an instant she had swept Judith's hair up and secured it with springy, sparkling clips. She teased out little fronds at her cheeks and nape. It gave Judith a gamine look.

Inspired, Kelly fetched her make-up bag and made Judith remove her spectacles. Then she sat her down and went to work, saying, 'You're not to peep until I've finished.'

Judith didn't much like people fiddling with her hair, and had never had a facial or massage, or been given advice on the use of cosmetics. She was certain she'd look like a clown, overpainted and ridiculous. Better the devil she knew than the one she didn't, and this included Peter. He'd hate it, she was sure.

'Peter doesn't like me to do anything different,' she said.

'Don't talk,' Kelly ordered, working a trace of blusher into Judith's cheek area. 'You're not still worrying about that relationship-type thing you've got with him, surely?'

Judith tried to nod without moving. Maybe it was

just as well that she was forbidden to speak. What she had to say on the subject was a pack of lies anyway. It was time she faced up to it. She wanted someone more exciting than Peter.

She looked down at the extraordinary spectacle of her nipples lifting the jersey fabric, and then further to her knees, wantonly displayed as the skirt rode up, straining over her thighs. Even her severe, lace-up shoes did not detract from the overall effect of repressed sluttery.

The gusset of her cotton drawers was uncomfortably damp. Every thought of Adam, and they came thick and fast, made her ache inside and caused a fresh infusion of love juice. The bedroom had an intimate ambience. She had envied the companionship of some of the girls at university, and had never had a close friend before. She was on a high, admiring Kelly hugely, wanting to express that admiration in physical terms, to touch her perhaps, or kiss her, yet shocked by such a notion.

Kelly worked like an artist, absorbed in her creation. 'I feel like Pygmalion,' she said happily. 'You're never going to believe this. You can look now.' And with a final flourish of pressed powder, she spun Judith round until she faced the cheval glass.

'Good heavens!' If Judith had been into swearing, her astonishment would have been couched in crude language.

She wasn't wearing her glasses, but could see herself clearly. Not even her own mother would have recognised her, maybe not Peter either, and he knew her much better. The girl in the mirror had a pointed, kittenish face. Her eyes were huge, slightly slanting up at the outer corners, outlined with kohl, the lashes lengthened and thickened with mascara, the lids smeared with greenish-blue shadow. It could have been garish, but was subtly executed. Her hair was spiked high and skewered to her head, wispy bits brushing her rouged cheeks and caressing the tender back of her neck.

Kelly had untied the towel pinned over the T-shirt to protect it, and Judith's breasts seemed larger. 'You need a new bra,' Kelly commented. 'Mine are too big or I'd lend you one. We'll get one, or maybe three, before we go to work in the morning. You can put it on in the ladies'. Don't want to spoil the effect when Adam gets his first sight of you.'

'I can't go out looking like this,' Judith wailed, afraid of hurting Kelly's feelings, but shy. Yet, deep within, she was eager to test her new persona.

'I'll tone down the foundation for daylight, if you like. You'll have to come sunbathing with me when the weather permits. There's nothing like a healthy tan. Dab a bit of sheen over it, dust on a few sparkles and you're as fit as a Cannes Film Festival starlet. Go for it, Judith. What have you got to lose? Oh, and when you get your first pay packet, why don't you invest in contact lenses, or a different pair of specs? Can you see without them?'

'Yes,' Judith admitted, still bemused. 'But I need them for reading. I'm long sighted.'

'We'll have to get up that bit earlier tomorrow, so I can do you,' Kelly said, picking up her cosmetics. 'Later, I'll show you how, then you'll be independent. The choice out there is amazing. You'll soon amass your own lip-liners and eye shadows, and all these gorgeous things that can turn a girl into something fabulous. Good night, Judith, and good hunting tomorrow.'

When Kelly had gone, Judith went into the bathroom and washed her face. Her own features emerged, but now they didn't seem quite so uninteresting. Kelly had opened a Pandora's Box and Judith would never feel the same about herself again.

She lay in bed with the reading lamp on, staring at the ceiling. Street noises drifted in at the half-opened window. It was turning-out time at the pub on the corner. She could hear male voices with that slightly out-of-control edge that proclaimed them as over the limit. She was glad to be tucked up in bed, rather than out on the street. She had never been able to cope with a gang of drunks, even at university when the students had over-indulged. Loud voices unnerved her.

She turned her thoughts to the Falcon Bookshop and what lay ahead. Though she had categorically denied it, she was interested in Adam. Drifting into sleep, his face was there to haunt her, obscuring others – Peter, the dream hero Marcus.

Giving a little moan, she didn't fight it, her hand slipping between her thighs, cupping the soft fleece as she permitted herself to let her imagination soar. And it was Adam cradling her mons . . . Adam bringing her to completion, not herself.

'And *was* she framed?' Adam said, smiling as he scrutinised Judith's T-shirt. She immediately regretted wearing it, for it drew too much attention to her breasts.

'Who?' she asked, feeling the blush rising, hating this uncontrollable show of embarrassment.

'Eve, of course. I presume that's what is meant. I'm inclined to agree. She's been given bad press down the ages. My namesake wimpishly blamed his fall from grace on her, with the pathetic excuse, "The woman tempted me." '

'They've been doing it ever since,' Kelly cut in caustically. 'Eve should have shacked up with the serpent, like Lilith, Adam's first wife.'

'Did he have one? I didn't know. She isn't mentioned in the Bible,' Judith exclaimed, hardly knowing what she was saying, hot under Adam's teasing regard. This was all getting too involved. She was there to work, not get mixed up in a theological discussion that had sexual undertones. She changed the subject, saying, 'Where d'you want me to start, Mr Renald?'

'By making coffee,' he replied, his eyes twinkling. Then he looked at Kelly and said, 'I've already switched on the computer. Do you know about setting up a website?'

'You bet,' she replied confidently, slanted him a glance and headed for the office.

It was a day like no other Judith had experienced, a busy day, with a steady flow of shoppers, a series of telephone calls and, in between, Adam showing her how to use the till, where to search for requested titles, and how to deal with awkward customers. The tourist season was just beginning and her command of French and German stood her in good stead, though most of the foreign visitors spoke English.

Working in such close proximity with Adam was stimulating and disturbing. She admired his panache, his knowledge and his way with people. When he chose, he could charm the birds right out of the trees. She didn't see Kelly all morning, as she was deeply engrossed with the computer.

At lunchtime, Adam told them to take a break; he would mind the shop and, as was his habit, had sandwiches delivered from the nearest café.

'Sheer laziness on my part,' he confided to Judith.

'My apartment is upstairs. Perhaps you'd like to see it some time?'

She went red once again. It seemed that she'd done little but blush every time he addressed her directly. She needed to get away from him, and dashed out with Kelly, grabbed a salad roll and cup of tea, then reluctantly agreed to a sprint round the department stores to look for underwear. They hadn't had time to do it before starting work.

Kelly homed in on a set of panties, bra and garter belt in black lycra and lace, then found another in scarlet. 'These will do for a start,' she said gleefully. 'Moderately priced, too. Later, when you've money to burn, you can go for the Janet Reger lingerie. Into the changing room and get them on.'

Fortunately it was deserted and Judith huddled in one of the cubicles and undressed. She hung her clothes on a peg and stepped into the alarmingly minute briefs, then adjusted the bra round her breasts and fastened the suspenders to the tops of her stockings. The long narrow glass threw back an image, but who was that brazen hussy in black underwear, breasts jacked high, nipples showing, fronds of dark pubic floss curling each side of the tiny panties?

'Come out,' ordered Kelly.

'Are you sure we're alone?' Judith said anxiously.

'Yes, yes. This is the fun part, seeing yourself from all angles in the mirrors.'

'I've seen myself and I'm not sure this sort of thing is really me.'

'I'll be the judge of that.'

Judith stepped through the curtains, feeling more exposed than if she'd been entirely nude. Kelly wolf-whistled and paced round her slowly. Four Judiths were reflected, each a daring image of a girl in provocative underclothes. There was a look in Kelly's eyes that somehow reminded Judith of Peter's when he was feeling horny.

'What d'you think? Should I return them?' she asked, hoping Kelly would say yes.

'Don't you dare,' Kelly answered softly, and reached out to touch Judith's bare nipples, that poked over the lacy edge of the bra cup. 'Clasp your hands behind your head. That's it. Your tits look gorgeous, raised up and pressed together. What a cleavage!' And she ran a finger down the deep V, then returned to caressing the nipples.

The old Judith wanted to step back, but the new wanton one leaned forward, chasing the pleasure darting from her nipples to her clitoris. She had never been touched so intimately by a woman before, but Kelly's fingers sent a frisson through her. She felt vulnerable with her arms strained up, but didn't dare move them. It was as if Kelly had bound her wrists with invisible chains.

Kelly's mouth was close, her face soft against Judith's. Then their lips met in a chaste kiss, but at the same time Kelly's hand cruised down between them and enclosed the black triangle that barely hid Judith's plump mound. Judith stayed still, fighting a losing battle with her arousal. It was just as well she hadn't removed the protective plastic from the gusset or she'd have creamed the fabric. Not that it mattered. She had no intention of putting the panties back. They were hers now, a part of her persona. She'd never wear sensible white cotton knickers again.

She sighed against Kelly's lips and, in answer, Kelly's middle finger gently traced the parting of Judith's labial wings. Then she withdrew both hand and mouth, smiling as she murmured huskily, 'Not now. Soon I'll show you how sweet it can be when girls make love.'

Judith was too surprised to reply and instead asked Kelly to pay while she put her T-shirt and skirt on over the glamorous bra and briefs, stuffing her old ones into the carrier bag. Kelly acted as if nothing untoward had taken place, rushing her back to the bookshop, then disappearing in the direction of the office and her beloved computer. But the dynamics had shifted subtly, and Judith knew things would never be quite the same between them again.

Kelly did not push it, however, announcing that she was going out that night with Caroline and Sally. 'The StingRayz are gigging in Bristol, and I thought I'd drive over and shag Alden again.'

'Oh,' Judith said, and found that she didn't relish an evening spent alone or, more likely, with Peter, who'd want to know the ins and outs of the Falcon Bookshop, complete with a full dossier on Adam Renald.

'D'you want to come along?' Kelly added, but very much as an afterthought.

'No thanks. It's not my kind of music.'

'I know. You're a culture vulture.'

'Who is?' asked Adam, entering the office after locking up.

'Judith,' said Kelly carelessly, slinging her tote bag over her shoulder. 'We're great mates but don't share the same taste in music.'

'Do you like piano works ... Chopin and Liszt?' Adam asked, almost eagerly.

'Oh, yes. Very much.' And Judith could hear the music as she spoke; the Preludes, the dreamy Nocturnes, the Sonatas, the romanticism of the two great composers and pianists.

'They were treated like rock stars, you know,' he put

in. 'The early Victorian ladies swooned over them, for they were handsome and wildly talented. Liszt was notorious for his love affairs, and gossip inferred that he was a Satanist. Chopin scandalised French society by living with Georges Sand, the novelist. She was considered to be no better than she should be, due to the fact that she had left her husband and liked to dress like a man and smoke cigars.'

'So there's nothing new under the sun?' Kelly commented, sarcastically.

'I think not,' he replied. 'So how about it, Judith? I've a couple of CDs I'd like you to hear. Come to the flat and listen now, and then I'll take you out to dinner.'

It was on the tip of her tongue to refuse, but rebellion flared up and she thought: why not? She was mad about music, and the idea of listening with a man who obviously shared her passion was a very appealing one. It wasn't often she found a fellow music-lover. This would be a rare treat indeed.

'All right,' she said, flushing with pleasure rather than embarrassment for once. 'Thank you.'

'See you later,' Kelly shouted as she went out of the door. 'Don't do anything I wouldn't. That should give you loads of leeway.' Her departure left a sense of emptiness behind.

'Shall we?' said Adam, and Judith followed where he led.

It was like living in a fairytale, walking through an enchanted forest in the company of a prince. Oh dear, Judith sighed, and scolded herself for such abject and ridiculous sentimentality. All that had happened was that her boss had asked her up to listen to his CDs and, very considerately, had invited her out to dinner. No big deal.

The apartment was spacious and, she thought, quite grand. It didn't have the neglected air of most bachelor pads. He must have someone in to do the cleaning, she concluded, as he motioned her to a deeply cushioned settee, and turned his attention to the stack of CDs.

For an hour Judith was transported to heaven. She had almost forgotten how inspiring she found Chopin's ballades and Liszt's études. The themes came flooding back. Her great-aunt had been a concert pianist and, when little, Judith had spent many happy hours under the Steinway grand piano in her drawing-room, while she thundered away overhead, the child's soul filling up with musical sounds.

Tears rose in Judith's eyes and she ached with emotion. It seemed so natural and right when Adam put an arm round her shoulders and offered her his handkerchief. She dabbed her eyes and thought of the black underwear that still felt alien against her skin. It was odd to be there, alone with him, in this splendid room with its state-of-the-art stereo equipment. His bedroom couldn't be far away, and hot scenarios flashed in her brain, of her in his arms, of him penetrating her, of sleeping with him, lulled by wonderful sounds.

He put on another CD, the notes tinkling like a mountain stream, then bursting into a firework display of dazzling arpeggios. He sat beside her and his hand came to rest on her knee. Judith froze.

It was inevitable, of course, but she was disappointed. She had hoped he would give her time, not hassle her into anything. To her relief he did nothing else. Then he took his hand away and stroked her cheek. 'Not crying any more?' he said tenderly.

'They were happy tears,' she murmured, her skin responding to his touch, her heart pounding, her insides melting like pink blancmange. She had never, ever experienced anything like this with Peter. Adam had found her Achilles heel.

'I know how you feel. I often wish I'd stuck at it and become a pianist,' he said, and kept his arm resting on the back of the couch, almost at her shoulders. 'I must introduce you to one of my friends. His name is Damian Cresswell, and he's also a collector. But he plays like a professional. You really must hear him.'

'I'd love to,' she sighed, willing to follow him to hell and back if need be.

'I'll arrange it,' he promised, then stood up and said, 'I don't know about you, but I'm starving. Let's go and eat. Oh, and Judith . . .'

'Yes, Adam,' she whispered, not quite used to calling him by his Christian name.

'Will you come back here afterwards? We could listen to more music.'

'Perhaps, Adam, if it's not getting too late,' she agreed, and every nerve in her body seemed to light up. The black panties caressed her hips and mons as she rose, and her nipples tingled against the lacy cups that upheld her breasts.

Chapter 4

'*GET TO KNOW HER*. Lull her into a false sense of security, then bring her to me,' Damian had said earlier that day, his tone no less commanding over the phone.

'Which one?' Adam had replied, wondering if he dare ask to speak to Anna.

'The shy girl, of course,' Damian had snapped impatiently. 'The other will join us, too, but she sounds more feisty. You know I take delight in initiating virgins and corrupting inexperienced young ladies. Do you think she has a virgin arse?'

'I can't say, master, but I would imagine so,' Adam had faltered, lust hammering at his groin. They had so much to offer, Anna and Damian, so many opportunities for taking part in debauchery. Just to speak to them from a distance was enough to give Adam an erection.

'Find out. I suggest you act at once. Then arrange for her to visit me.'

'Yes, master,' Adam had said, and set about planning Judith's seduction.

There's a world of difference between dining in a select restaurant with a man who knows his cuisine, and a yobbo who thinks that taking a girl to get a Chinese take-away is pushing the boat out, Judith concluded, watching Adam with growing admiration.

She wished she was wearing something other than the clothes she'd been in all day, but her new underwear made her feel special. Adam was still casually dressed, though he had buttoned down his collar and added a tie. His old school one? she pondered. His manner of speech, his ease when consulting the menu or ordering wine, pointed to a quality education.

The Haunch of Venison was an ancient coaching inn, and it had steadily built a reputation for food that was second to none. Judith sat with Adam in an oak-panelled room where horse brasses glittered. There was a huge chimney-breast and open hearth, and logs smouldered between the andirons, the heap of powdery ash suggesting that the fire hadn't been allowed to go out all winter.

She had enjoyed the short walk from the shop, for it was a mild, dry evening; she was finding everything she did with him an adventure. Usually she shrank into herself on entering a bar, but it was different when escorted by a man such as Adam. Porters opened doors for them, waiters jumped to attention. Adam's bearing gave him clout wherever he went. And this spread to her. Just for tonight, she was his lady. She liked the feeling of regality.

'This inn was already old when Chaucer wrote *The Canterbury Tales*,' he vouchsafed, nodding to the wine waiter to refill their glasses. 'It has a reputation for being haunted. Do you feel a ghostly presence?'

Judith glanced round, but all she could see were couples like themselves relaxing in the convivial atmosphere, or businessmen with their heads together concluding deals. 'No, nothing,' she said, smiling at him nervously. She was more in awe of him than of any apparition.

'You see the fireplace over there?' he went on, nodding in its direction. 'Well, when they were opening it up not so long ago, they found a skeletal hand buried in the wall. The bony fingers were clenched round a pack of cards. A sharp, perhaps, caught cheating? It was a small hand . . . could have been a woman's.'

'How horrible,' she said with a shudder.

'It's on show in the local museum, if you want to see it,' he added cheerfully, spearing a portion of smoked trout on the tines of his fork before transferring it to his mouth.

'No, thank you. I'd rather not,' she said, shaking her head and concentrating on her salad starter.

The wine was red and strong, and she could already feel it going to her head. The main course arrived, succulent, melt-in-the-mouth steaks in garlic sauce, served with French fries and mushrooms. Adam was in full flow, disobeying the rule about talking with the mouth full. She listened with half her mind, more concerned about using the correct cutlery and consuming the food without making an idiot of herself.

'So you see, if I can get all my stock on the Net, it should encourage sales. Besides which, with Kelly's help, I can log on to the market that deals with more salacious subjects. Prints and photographs similar to mine. Did you know that there are only eight hundred pornographic daguerreotypes known to be in existence? Two hundred of those belong to one collector. They're worth about ten thousand pounds each.'

Judith remembered the pictures very well, and the models who had probably been prostitutes. There had been one in particular that had caught her imagination. It was that of a mature woman with her skirts up, bare from the waist to her stocking tops. Her legs were spread wide, her bush, sex lips and protruding clitoris fully displayed to a young, uniformed army officer who was staring down at it in amazement. It was spicy stuff, the participants seemingly unaware of the camera, as if caught in a private moment.

'You're thinking about them, aren't you?' Adam said suddenly, setting down his wine glass.

'Well, yes . . . I was,' she confessed. 'I didn't know such explicit pictures were taken in those days.'

'A great deal of erotica was produced in Paris in the 1840s and 50s. It appealed to the gentlemen far more than art . . . the unstructured reality; casual, natural, not even posed. You could buy a woman for five francs, but that was soon over. With a photograph the voyeur could go on looking at it again and again, masturbating if he wanted. What value for money.'

'But wasn't it limited to a wealthy few?' Judith squeaked, trying to appear sophisticated, but losing her composure at his mention of solitary sex.

'In the beginning, but it soon spread and became popular with the middle market. Dirty photos could be bought in every slightly downbeat location . . . the rail stations, the streets, the flea markets. The police got wind of it, and it was seen as a powerful, subversive force, and driven underground by 1855.'

'I never realised,' Judith exclaimed, trying to pretend that they were having a perfectly normal conversation. 'History is so interesting.'

'And the most astonishing thing is that people don't change. There was porn then and there's porn now. It's branched off and expanded, that's all, available on the

70

Internet as well as in blue movies. Our ancestors would have loved the chatrooms. Don't you?'

'I've never gone into one,' Judith admitted, freezing in her seat as she felt his hand creeping up her leg and landing in her lap. 'I haven't a computer, and neither has Kelly.'

'No? I'll have to do something about that. Can't have my staff denied access to the very latest in filth.'

'I wouldn't want to look,' she declared stoutly. Now his finger was pressing down, finding the opening between the buttons of her front-fastening skirt.

'No? Aren't you in the least bit curious to watch others performing sex? Men with men, perhaps, or girls bringing each other to orgasm? Maybe a heterosexual couple having it away? Can you truly sit there and tell me you haven't wanted to see what they do, how they do it, and when?' His voice was low, hypnotic, and his finger wormed its way in, tickling her naked belly and finding the edge of her panties.

'I . . . I haven't . . . I'm not that interested,' she stammered.

'Really? Then you must be damn near the only one in the world who isn't. Sex sells, my dear, in any shape or form.'

Judith felt a sense of outrage and crippling shame as his fingertip teased her pubic hair. She pushed his hand away, saying, 'Mr Renald . . . Adam . . . please!'

He grinned into her face. 'Please stop, or please continue?' he teased.

'Stop. We . . . hardly . . . know each other,' she stuttered. 'It's too soon. And here, in the middle of a restaurant . . . well, really!'

He pulled a contrite face, then raised his finger and sniffed it. 'You smell delicious,' he said, and took her hand and caressed the palm with his thumb, an action calculated to cause a furore inside her. 'I'm sorry. I must have misread your signals. I thought we were getting along fine and had so much in common.'

'We are . . . we have. Oh, don't think I'm not happy in your company. I am, very much so, but I wouldn't want you to think I'm a push-over, a cheap and easy lay.'

'Oh, Judith, I'll never think that,' he vowed, and lifted her hand to his lips, hovering over the back of it, not quite kissing it, the warmth of his breath raising the fine down on her skin. 'I didn't mean to offend you.'

She felt immensely guilty all of a sudden, as if she had hurt this kind, caring man. 'You haven't. I've really enjoyed myself this evening. But now I'd better go. I don't want to miss the last bus to Castleford.'

'But you haven't had pudding. I refuse to let you leave until you've tasted their finest. Believe me, they make the most ravishing desserts. Afterwards, you might care to come back to the flat and I'll order you a cab. What d'you say? Am I forgiven for being insensitive?'

What could she say but yes? When Adam pulled out all the stops it would have taken a saint to resist him.

The pudding was as promised. There was a choice of apricots stewed in brandy, profiteroles stuffed with whipped cream and swimming in melted chocolate, and gateau with glacé cherries and nuts. Adam leaned across at one point and removed a stray dab of confectionery from the corner of her lips, using his little finger.

' "Sweets for the sweet," ' he quoted, and transferred it to his own mouth, lapping it up with an air of thoughtless enjoyment, like a dog. Judith found this unpleasant and her misgivings returned. Then he said, 'I told you it wasn't to be missed, didn't I? Now, what say we skip coffee? I'll make some when we get to my place.'

He held her coat for her, and settled the bill, then tucked his hand under the crook of her elbow and walked her back to the shop. She knew it was unwise to delay, but the wine had got to her, and so had he. No doubt Kelly would have a risqué adventure to relate, and so, it seemed, would she.

Peter appeared briefly in her thoughts, and she momentarily regretted the fact that life couldn't be more simple. It would have been so easy to have become his fiancée and married him in due course. Yet every second spent with Adam was exciting. She recognised that she had never lit up for Peter as she was doing for her new boss. She was unsure of him, uncertain how far to go, what to do or say, half expecting him to dismiss her brusquely, ring for a taxi and send her home.

Instead, he seemed pleased that she had agreed to come, gesturing to his CDs and saying, 'You choose the music. What do you like?'

'Most things, except perhaps baroque,' she answered, going over and examining the stack, revolving it on the turntable. 'My, but you've a large collection,' she added.

There were pieces she knew and composers she didn't; symphonies and concertos, ballet music and double opera CDs. It was daunting, but she selected one near the top. Maybe he played this often. It was Rachmaninov's Piano Concerto Number 2.

'An excellent choice,' he said. 'Have you seen the film *Shine*?'

'Oh, yes,' she said, sitting down again and clasping

her arms round her knees. 'Wonderful playing. Such a compelling story as well.' Then she found herself thinking, I'll bet Kelly's not wasting time talking about music with Alden Ray. She's probably done it with him at least twice by now.

Adam didn't make coffee, but fetched more wine from the kitchen and served it in crystal flutes. They drank and listened to the Russian composer's masterpiece, then he put down his glass and said, 'Kiss me.'

He took his mouth to hers, and then his whole body, touching her slowly and then holding her tightly against him. She wanted to part her lips, but let him take over. He held her face in his hands and then drew his nails lightly down her hot cheek. He withdrew and looked at her.

'You're beautiful, Judith,' he said. 'Now relax, enjoy. Let me show you how it is when someone makes love to you.'

'I already have a boyfriend,' she said, amazed that he found her pleasing, striving to be fair to Peter, yet wanting him to go on kissing her. Her panties were soaking, and the black strip of lycra at the gusset had worked its way up between the vertical line of her swollen labia. She ached for him to touch her there, not only with his fingers, but also with his lips.

'And he satisfies you?' He sounded doubtful, lowering his hand to her female mound and touching it through the blue denim.

She wanted to lie, some misdirected feeling of loyalty to Peter almost making her distort the truth, but she couldn't. She had reached an epiphany, a blinding moment of insight, and she knew that whatever happened with Adam, she would no longer go on faking orgasm.

'No, he doesn't,' she said quietly.

'You've never climaxed?' His hand crept under her T-shirt, lifting it high and cupping her right breast. He squeezed gently, his thumbnail scratching across the nipple.

'I have – alone,' she confessed.

'So you know what your clitoris requires?'

'Oh, yes.'

He smiled, then bent to kiss each nipple through the black lace. Judith moaned and arched her spine, pushing her breasts against his mouth. She clutched at him, burying her hands in his dark hair, and he slipped a hand under her skirt again, parted her legs and moved up the length of her thigh. Judith was so aroused that she imagined the slightest touch on her clit-head would shoot her to the peak. He kneaded her pubis as he had done her breasts, then pushed aside her panties and rubbed the soft, brown bush.

'Is that nice?' he murmured, and passed his tongue round the rim of her ear, making her shiver.

'Oh, yes,' she sighed, hardly able to form the words, almost oblivious to anything but the combination of his tongue in her ear and his finger between her sex lips, locating her bud and beginning that slow stroking motion that would bring on her orgasm.

'I'm going to take you through to my bedroom. We'll be more comfortable there,' he said, and she wanted to cry with frustration, suddenly bereft of his tongue and hands.

She stumbled along with his arm looped over her shoulders. The apartment was large, the décor tasteful, the furniture chosen to suit the old-world ambience, but it also had the benefit of a modern central heating system. Adam led her along a short corridor and into a large room. Like the rest of his home, it had William Morris wallpaper, elegant friezes and furniture from the beginning of the last century. The bed dominated everything: a large, velvet-hung tester, with brass posts at foot and head. Adam guided her towards it. Her feet dragged unwillingly, but her body was driving her on.

'Gosh!' she exclaimed, clinging desperately to her cool. 'It's like something out of an Edwardian TV drama.'

'I'm a man of my time, but I appreciate the craftsmanship of a bygone age,' he replied, and leaned a hand against one of the posts. 'It's rock solid and never shakes, no matter what takes place within it.'

'You're not married, are you?'

He laughed and shook his head. 'Not on your sweet life, and this is more like a bed for three or even four persons, don't you think?'

She didn't know what to think, mesmerised by his handsome face, his untidy curls and lean body, imagining him naked, bending over her while she lay on that enormous couch. Would he do the thing that she had been longing for? Was it possible that he'd kiss her breasts, her navel and go lower, finally licking her bud? Her breath shortened and she swayed towards him. He caught her and held her and said, 'I shall undress you, and then show you paradise.'

With slow deliberation he lifted the T-shirt up and over her head. His eyes shone and his mouth set in a sensual line as he perused her breasts in the provocative bra. Then he unbuttoned her skirt and let it drop, kicking it aside with his foot. Judith resisted the impulse to place an arm across her breasts and a hand over her mons. She had bought this lingerie with the intention of showing it off, hadn't she? No use turning chicken now.

Adam stepped closer and slid his hands under the shoulder straps, then pulled them down, her breasts popping up from the wired cups. He stared at her hard, rose-pink nipples. Reaching around her, he unhooked the fastening and the bra fell away. Judith took a deep breath, lifted her ribs and made her breasts jut out. In for a penny, in for a pound, she thought, but didn't know what she really meant – only that there was no turning back. She sat on the bed and Adam unlaced her shoes and took them off, then he unclipped her stockings and rolled them down and removed the garter belt. He was so neat and adept that she realised he must have undressed many women before her.

He pushed her down on the bed, winding his fingers in her hair and saying, 'Have you ever wanted to hand yourself over to another, stronger person?'

Truth time, she reminded herself, and said, 'I daydream of swashbuckling heroes sometimes. They always master me, but give me the most exquisite pleasure.'

'Masturbation fantasies?'

'I guess,' she quavered.

'I'm going to give you a choice, my dear,' he went on, and ran his thumbs under the ribbon ties of her panties, undid them, and slowly eased the fabric over her pubis. 'We can either have straightforward, missionary position, vanilla sex, like you do with your boyfriend ... or you can submit your will to me. Which is it to be?'

'I don't like losing control,' she protested, while deep in her psyche something dark and forbidden started to awaken. Oh, to be helpless and unable to prevent another person performing all the wildest desires and fantasies she had ever dreamed up.

'You won't be out of control. I shan't do anything you don't want – deep down inside, that is. I can give you a safe word, if you like, to stop me if you think I'm going too far. How about "dangerous"? Do you dare accept my challenge?'

'Yes, Adam,' she said.

He seized and held her with arms outspread. Before she realised what he was doing, he bound silk scarves round her wrists, drew them tight and tied the free ends to each of the posts at the bedhead. He straddled her as he did this, pressing down and making her aware of the erection tenting his chinos. It was still there when he spread out her legs and slipped manacles on her ankles, then chained them to the foot of the bed. The fur-lined cuffs didn't hurt, but the feeling of restriction was unusual, not unpleasant and certainly exciting.

'Well done, darling. You passed the first test with honours,' he said, his eyes bright. 'How do you like it, eh? You can't move, can you? I can do anything I like with you. I'm your master.'

Judith cried out as he lowered his face to her breasts, his tongue flicking over her erect nipples. She tugged at her bonds, but it was useless. He continued to suckle at her, his teeth nipping playfully. Pleasure saturated her, pooling in her sex, yet not enough to bring on her crisis.

'Please,' she gasped. 'Please, please . . . I've always wanted . . . never dared to ask . . .'

'You want me to fuck your arse?'

'No! That's sounds horrible. But I'd like you to lick me . . . there, between the legs.'

'Dear, dear, we are a horny little slut, aren't we?' he teased. 'Has no one gone down on you before?'

'No,' she whispered, flushing all over.

'I think you deserve a spanking for such impure thoughts.'

She hadn't bargained for that, but was given no choice. Adam's hand came down hard on her thighs and belly. His blows stung and she yelped, but didn't use the safe word. Pain darted through her, but also a frenzied sort of pleasure.

Adam stopped, stood by the bed and unzipped his fly, exposing an impressively swollen cock. As Judith watched, he massaged it from base to helm, caressing the shaft and smearing the glans with the pre-come seeping from its eye. Leaving it sticking out like a spear from the thicket of wiry pubic hair, he shrugged off his jacket and shirt, exposing a body that was well toned and bore no trace of superfluous fat. Judith gulped and her clit spasmed. She had never seen a more splendid example of masculinity – not in real life, anyway.

His trousers slid down, fully exposing his cock, that swayed as he moved, jutting above the swollen balls in their wrinkled sac. Judith ached to lip it, and her clitoris throbbed as she imagined taking it into her mouth as far as it would go. Then she would suck him hard, milking him of his last drop of semen.

Now he was as naked as she and, kneeling over her, he rubbed the tip of his cock between her breasts, shifting so that each nipple was wet with his juice. His thighs gripped her at each side, and he lifted his hips, using his cock like a paint-brush, bedewing her chin, her nose and mouth, her eyelids. Judith felt dizzy with desire, trying to take him in her mouth, but refused the privilege, bucking with her hips, but unable to move more than an inch or two off the mattress.

'Impatient,' he chided softly, and his touch on her pubis quietened her, as if he had put her under a spell.

He slithered lower and lipped her thighs, pressing little kisses down her legs. He came to her ankles, and licked them, then turned his attention to her toes, sucking each one diligently, as if it was a miniature penis. Wave after wave of glorious feeling coursed through her, gathering in her clit but not satisfying it. She moaned as he sat between her thighs, bending her knees so that they flopped apart as far as her bonds would allow. He bent and pushed his tongue into her navel, circling and playing with it. She could no longer suppress her need, whimpering and writhing. He was so near to doing what she'd dreamed of – but would he?

He smiled at her, then pressed his mouth to her furry mound. Judith started, the stab of pleasure acute. 'Be still,' he cautioned, and ran his tongue across her wet cleft, then found her nubbin and sucked it.

Judith was on fire, his slaps, his careful arousing of her body, bringing her up and up, rising towards that precious plateau. She was anxious, mindful of her needy clit, wishing she could touch it herself and ensure completion. Supposing Adam stopped at the last minute, leaving her suspended betwixt heaven and hell?

To her intense joy, he reached up with both hands and found her nipples, rolling them between his fingers, tripling her ecstasy. Her orgasm was so strong that she thought her body might disintegrate. The spasms went on and on, undulating through her, and she wanted so much to grab him and hold him tight, to wind herself in and around him.

It seemed he had picked up on her thoughts when he released the scarves and manacles that held her captive, rolled her over on to her stomach and put an arm under her, hauling her to her knees, bottom in the air. She felt his fingers penetrate her, first one, then two. He wiggled them around, massaging her inner walls and making her thoroughly wet. She moaned, feeling the pressure just behind her clitoris, and longed to have his stiff cock pushing its way up there. Then he removed his fingers and took them to her tiny, virgin nether hole, smearing her juice around it, sticking the tip of a finger inside.

'Oh, please don't,' she said, flinching.

'You don't like being rimmed, not even like this?' he asked, and leaned down, running his tongue round her puckered anus.

'No. Well, I don't think so. It feels odd ... unnatural,' she said, but was aware of a tingling sensation and the perverse desire to have him explore her secrets further.

'How about this?' he asked softly, and rubbed his cock-head up and around her anal entrance. Then he pushed, ever so slightly, but enough to make her shoot forward to avoid him.

'No!' she yelled. 'I don't like it!'

'OK. No need to panic,' he soothed, and moved her round until she lay on her back. He kissed her deeply, then had her embrace him with her legs, lifting them and resting her ankles on each of his shoulders to give him greater access.

He was no longer controlled, covering her roughly, his penis entering her forcefully. She was aware that he wore a sheath. Looking down between her belly and his body, she glimpsed his thick phallus shrouded in black rubber pumping in and out of her, faster and faster, until he finally erupted. He collapsed on her, his face buried in her hair, his spent organ slipping from her channel.

Kelly felt the need to watch out for Judith – even more so since she had confessed to having been fucked by Adam. That's exactly how it had sounded when a starry-eyed Judith told her about it next day. He had spanked, dominated and finally fucked her. There had been no question of Judith being the top. Oh no. Adam Renald relished that position by the sound of things.

Warning bells clanged in Kelly's head. She knew enough about S&M to understand where he was coming from. Judith was taking it so seriously, turning it into a romantic love thing. Kelly wanted to warn her not to read too much into it, but it seemed that Judith now looked upon her boss and herself as an item, and was tortured with remorse regarding Peter. As far as Kelly could tell, there was no change in Adam's attitude towards Judith during working hours.

For her own part, she was fully occupied with setting up the website and correlating the vast amount of stock in the shop. She planned to get everything on file: clients, booksellers, publishers, each and every enquiry. He had badly needed a computer nerd like her. But it meant she hadn't much opportunity to observe the lovebirds – or rather the lovesick hen. Whenever she happened to bump into Adam she let him know that she *knew*, and that if he messed her friend about she'd be wearing his bollocks as earrings. She didn't put this into words, but guessed that he'd got the message, though he was still looking infuriatingly smug.

Friday came, and Adam strolled into the office and said to Kelly, 'You've a car, haven't you?'

'I have, the faithful though tarty Tracy,' she replied, looking up from the screen. 'Why?'

'I need you to make a special delivery. Take Judith with you for back-up.'

Kelly twirled round in her operators' chair. 'What is it? The Crown Jewels?' she said, using the sarcastic tone that she couldn't keep from her voice when addressing him. It wasn't that she disliked him, but she had a gut feeling about him – one of distrust.

'No, a set of rare photographs.'

'Is it far?'

'Twenty miles.'

'Are they for a customer? Can't they collect themselves? This isn't very cost-effective, you know. When your site is up and running, you'll have to do better than this. I suggest a credit card arrangement.'

'I didn't ask for your opinion on how I conduct my business,' he said briskly.

Kelly let her skirt ride up, just to see his reaction. It was satisfactory. His eyes fixed on her bare thigh and the package behind his fly enlarged. She smiled, and ran a finger thoughtfully over her pouting lower lip in a baby-doll kind of way that few men could resist. She had to admit that she was bored. The second backstage shag with Alden had proved a let down. Though the band had blown the Colston Hall apart, she felt she wouldn't be following them any more, feeling that she had matured and passed beyond the StingRayz and their self-obsessed lead singer.

'When d'you want me to make the drop?' she asked, casually passing a hand over nipples that lifted the black jersey fabric of her crop-top. The ring in her navel glinted.

'This evening, after work,' he said, and came to stand behind her, looking at the page on the monitor. 'Don't worry. You'll get overtime. I don't expect you to do it for nothing.'

Kelly clicked the mouse. At once the name of the shop flashed up, followed by the gradual unfolding of a picture of its frontage, and material concerning both Adam and his collection.

'There you go,' she said. 'It's on the hard disc and a

floppy. Even a terminally untalented computer illiterate wouldn't be able to bin it.'

'It's brilliant,' he responded, and rested his hands on her shoulders.

'Not finished yet, but we're getting there,' she said, then, without taking her gaze from the screen, added, 'Please move your hands.'

'You don't like me touching you?' He sounded incredulous, but did as she requested.

'I like to set boundaries. I work for you. That's the bottom line. I decide if it goes any further.'

'No problem,' he said, then lapsed back into silence.

'Now that we're on the subject, I'm warning you, Adam. If you hurt Judith, you're dead,' she said in a low, even voice, still working the mouse.

'I get the message.'

'Good.'

'But I haven't seen you all week. I thought it would be easier when you moved in with Kelly,' Peter grumbled. 'Can't I come round tonight. I could bring a video and we could order a pizza.'

They were talking on the phone and Judith was thankful that there was no video link. She'd been avoiding him for days, filled with the most wickedly exciting combination of guilt, shame and lust. Adam hadn't repeated his actions in the apartment, in fact he had been almost cool, but she put this down to his gentlemanly desire to shield her from gossip. He would ask her out again when he thought it was politic to do so. She admired his chivalry and was rather lofty when Kelly made a disparaging remark. And now Peter was jabbering away down the line and wanting her to spend the weekend with him. She was rather hoping that Adam might suggest another dinner engagement, or a cosy evening spent listening to music and making love.

As she thought about this, her bottom warmed. What was it that medical men said? The skin remembers traumas. Did hers recall Adam's slaps? Seated on the settee, telephone to her ear, she could feel her nipples chafing against her scarlet bra and was aware of love juice soaking into her panties. The thought of being spanked aroused her almost as much as the desire to have him thrust into her again.

'Sorry, Peter, but Kelly and me have to run an errand for the shop. There's a valuable item to be taken to a customer.'

'But that won't take all night, surely? Where is it? Up in the stratosphere, or on one of Jupiter's moons?' When Peter attempted irony, he only succeeded in sounding peevish. Judith found this intensely irritating.

'It's in Druids Mill village. At the Rectory. Somewhere between here and Bath,' she said, then added something that she immediately regretted. 'Why don't you come along for the ride? We can stop off at a pub on the way back.'

'And spend the night together?' he asked eagerly.

'What about your mum?'

'She's gone to see my auntie in Weston-super-Mare.'

Bugger it, Judith thought. Now how am I going to avoid sleeping with him? I know – I'll tell him I'm on. That's what Kelly would do. I'm getting more like her by the minute.

'Oh, Jesus, do we really have to take him?' Kelly groaned when Judith broke the news. 'He's such a drag.'

'Sorry, but I couldn't very well avoid it,' Judith said,

contritely. 'I don't want him to guess about Adam. Though I suppose I'll have to tell him soon.'

'Tell him what? That you humped Adam . . . once?'

'It'll happen again. I know there's something strong between us.' Judith spoke so vehemently that Kelly suspected her of harbouring doubts.

'If you say so, hon,' she said, giving in. There was no use arguing with someone so infatuated. Best to leave it to karma, or fate, or plain old common sense, which would eventually prevail. Adam was a love-rat, of that Kelly was sure.

Tracy decided to behave for once, and they arrived at the Falcon Bookshop on time. Adam was outside, waiting for them, and he handed a parcel to Judith who was occupying the passenger seat beside Kelly. He glanced in and saw Peter in the back. Judith introduced them.

'Ah, pleased to meet you,' Adam said, with his charming smile. 'Judith's told me so much about you.'

Kelly noticed that Judith blushed to the roots of her hair. God, she'll never make an adulteress, she thought, Tracy purring under her hands, sounding almost eager to go for a spin.

All the time, Kelly was attuned to the tensions going on around her: Peter trying desperately to hide his jealousy and be hail-fellow-well-met to Adam; Adam as smooth as silk, and Judith in a welter of embarrassment and shame. Lord, what to do with them? Kelly thought, then took the bull by the horns, saying, 'All set, then? We really must go. People to see, things to do. See yah, Adam. 'Bye.'

They were off, Tracy skidding in her eagerness to get away. The miles bowled under the wheels, but there was an oppressive silence in the car after Peter had said, unnecessarily, 'So he's your boss, is he, Judith?'

86

'Yes,' she answered, huddled into herself, her hands clutching the parcel on her lap fiercely, as if it was one of Adam's children.

'He's a bit posh, isn't he? A bit of a girlish type. Is he a poof?'

'No,' Judith replied with rather too much emphasis. 'He isn't gay.'

'Looks like it, though. Long hair and that creepy manner. Bet he's a shirt-lifter and you don't know it.'

'Shut up, Peter,' Kelly said grittily. 'You wouldn't know a Martha from an Arthur, even if they wagged their dick in your face. Just shut up about something you don't understand. But I'll tell you this for free. He fucks women, and that's for sure. I know. I've done it.'

'With him? You haven't wasted any time,' Peter said ungraciously.

'You always did think I was a slut-girl. Well, now you know.'

Why am I doing this? Kelly pondered, pausing at a crossroads and then taking the right-hand fork, signposted Druids Mill. I know damn well that Judith would be better off without that dork hanging around. Keep out of it, Miss Cameron. Keep your great big hooter out of it and stop caretaking people. It's not your problem.

It was getting dark and the street-lights in the village shone yellow overhead. 'There's a pub,' Judith said, leaning forward and peering through the windscreen.

'I can see that, girl,' Kelly said, and then stopped at a side street where a sign said: THE RECTORY 2 MILES. 'Yippee!' she shouted. 'We're almost there, gang. No pubbing until we've safely delivered, and I can't have more than half of lager.'

The lane was sparsely lit, but they came to a pair of

high wrought-iron gates, which opened electronically to allow Tracy through. A beech-lined avenue stretched ahead, and at the end of it stood a large mansion, backed by gardens and sentinel trees. It had a pitched roof and narrow arched windows, and steps leading up to a front door that looked like the entrance to a mausoleum. Floodlights illumined the impressive façade, but even so the aspect was gloomy.

'Welcome to the House Of Usher,' Kelly intoned in a sepulchral voice, as she climbed out of the driver's door.

She was aware of Judith and Peter behind her as she advanced up the wide, shallow steps. She reached the top and was about to grab the brass bell-pull when the door opened, letting out a flood of light. A tall, beautiful woman was silhouetted there, her long chiffon skirt made transparent by the glow, outlining a magnificent pair of legs.

She held out her hands to Kelly, her palms cool, her nails almond-shaped and painted gold. 'You must have been sent by Adam,' she carolled, her tone mellifluous. 'Come in. Is that the parcel? Oh, Damian is going to be so pleased. He's in the music room, practising.'

They stood in the hall, tiled in black and white, with marble columns and alcoves containing statues, and Kelly could hear piano music thundering out from a room on the left.

'I'm Anna Cresswell,' the woman continued, even more lovely in the light from the chandeliers. Her features were perfect, her eyes amethyst, her hair a blonde, teased and high-lighted mane, and her body was lithe and graceful, with big breasts, prominent nipples, a tiny waist and rounded hips.

Kelly looked at her and wanted her, her appreciation of women, their minds, their souls and their sensual bodies increasing tenfold. Anna's scent seemed to reach out and enfold her; not only the expensive French perfume, but the subtle aroma of her skin, her hair and her pussy. Kelly wanted to lie down with her somewhere peaceful and beautiful and explore that marvellous body, drown in those eyes and die on that crimson mouth.

Chapter 5

THE MUSIC CAME TO a dramatic conclusion in a flurry of glissandos and sombre chords and, after a moment, a man appeared, passing under the ornamental lintel of the salon's cedarwood doors.

Judith couldn't believe her eyes. It was as if one of her make-believe heroes had suddenly materialised in solid flesh, blood, bone and muscle. Heathcliff incarnate, with maybe a dash of Count Dracula. The word 'charismatic' sprang to mind. It wasn't that he was extremely handsome – that went without saying – but there was another quality, one that froze her blood. Darkness called to darkness, her whole being responding. He had a lupine quality, with sherry-gold eyes that slanted slightly at the outer corners and a face that was almost Slavic, rather broad at the cheekbones. He didn't look English, but had no accent when he spoke, the cadence of his voice thrilling straight down to her sex, penetrating her as surely as if he had plugged her with his cock.

'Good evening,' he said, smiling as he approached. 'Adam phoned and told me you were coming. Are these the photographs, Anna?' She nodded and handed him the package. He did not undo it, but made an expansive gesture that included his visitors, adding, 'You'll stay to dinner, of course. I feel I may have ruined your plans for this evening.'

'That's quite all right,' Kelly answered, acting as their spokesperson. 'All part of the job, Mr Cresswell.'

'Please call me Damian,' he insisted, and Judith felt his gaze fall on her, his piercing eyes seeming to assess her beyond her physical self. 'And this is Anna, my cousin.'

'I've already introduced myself, darling,' she said, and moved across to stand at his side. There was a glamour about them that reminded Judith of royalty, or famous actors who were renowned as partners and co-stars. Who were they and where did they fit into the picture? If they were Adam's friends, then she must get to know them.

'I'm Judith Shaw,' she said, amazed by her own boldness. 'And this is Kelly Cameron, and a friend of mine, Peter Marsh.'

Within minutes she felt as if she had known Anna and Damian forever. If Adam had beguiled her, then it was as nothing compared to the wit, elegance and knack of putting people at ease that seemed to exude from the very pores of the cousins. She was utterly bowled over, and even the cynical Kelly and suspicious Peter succumbed.

First, they toured the ground floor of the house, with their host and hostess expounding on its age, history and the discoveries that had been made during restoration. It was high Gothic, and Judith could not help remembering her first impression of the distinguished-looking yet somewhat sinister Damian. Did he sleep in a coffin hidden away in a vault somewhere? She didn't see one, but there was a reception area as large as a ballroom; a library; a dining room; a games room complete with full-sized billiard table; and a noble conservatory reminiscent of those at Kew Gardens, filled with exotic tropical plants and trees.

'We made an addition of our own,' Damian said, as he led them through this jungle paradise to a domed space wherein lay a lagoon-shaped pool, tiled in azure and lit up from under the water.

The atmosphere was humid, and the torrid effect increased by squawks coming from a large aviary where parrots flaunted and flirted, performed acrobatics on branches and walked up and down the perches.

'How gorgeous!' Kelly cried, almost tempted to tear off her clothes then and there and dive into the water.

'Anna and I just had to have it. We're used to the sun and sea ... spend much of the year abroad. You may use it sometime, if you wish.'

Dinner was served in the conservatory, the table and rattan chairs reminiscent of the Raj, the heavily foliaged plants with their flamboyant blossoms harking back to the days when the Englishman or woman, sojourning in foreign climes, was treated as someone superior. The male servant, who the cousins addressed as Fadil, added to this impression, a dark-skinned man in a white high-buttoned jacket, straight trousers and a tasselled fez. Silent-footed, he brought in the dishes of superbly cooked food, assisted by a pretty woman in the traditional maid's uniform of short, full black taffeta skirt and frilly white apron.

There was no lack of conversation. Anna was vivacious and Damian possessed an unending repertoire of amusing and outrageous anecdotes concerning his travels.

'He's incorrigible,' Anna remarked, picking up her wine glass and sitting back in her chair, surveying

Peter from under curling lashes coated with mascara. There was a faintly mocking expression on her face. 'Tell me, Peter, are you anything to do with the book trade?'

Judith was intrigued by the way in which he shifted uncomfortably, his colour rising as he glanced at Anna. Was it simply that he was unaccustomed to dining with an intelligent, well-travelled couple? Or did he find Anna overwhelmingly attractive, and was worried by and ashamed of the desire rampaging through his body? Judith certainly was, when it came to Damian.

'No ... Anna. I make furniture,' he managed to answer.

'How interesting. I'd like to see it. Will you show me?' As she leaned closer to him, her cleavage became more apparent.

'You can visit my workshop any time,' he said, gazing longingly at that delicious display of flesh.

Judith wasn't exactly jealous, but it was vexing to be put in the shade by such a sexy woman. Anna might be a lady, possibly even titled, but she probably had alley-cat morals. Then Judith's attention was captured by Damian.

'You're not the computer buff, so you must be Adam's assistant,' he said.

'I am,' she answered, wanting to impress him but not sure how.

'And you've not long finished at university?'

'That's correct.'

'And what else do you like, besides musty old books?'

'Music,' she stated emphatically.

'Ah, so ... I, too,' he replied, and his hand lay alongside hers on the damask cloth. He didn't touch her, but the idea of those long, slender fingers drawing harmonies from the piano excited her more than if he had taken liberties with her body.

'Adam mentioned that you were a pianist.'

'I'll play for you after dinner,' he promised, and his wolfish eyes trapped hers. For a second she couldn't look away.

She had taken Kelly's advice and, now that work was finished, her spectacles were tucked in her handbag. She had to admit that they were more of a habit than a necessity, apart from when she wanted to read. However, she was conscious that her floral slip dress was too informal for dinner, but then neither Damian nor his cousin was wearing anything other than casual clothing.

Anna had on a low-necked blouse, ankle-length silk skirt and high-heeled strappy sandals. Damian was attired in skin-tight black leather trousers, the belt fastened by a silver buckle shaped like an eagle, and a black polo sweater. His bare feet were thrust into loafers, and he sat easily in his chair, taking up whatever pose was most comfortable; sometimes with one leg tucked under him or crossed at the knee. The food was fit for a king, Fadil deferential, as was Prunella, the maid, yet Damian and Anna might as well have been in a burger bar or on a picnic. They ate like Continentals, gesturing, snuggling close to their dinner companion, talking eagerly while eating, slurping at their glasses, non-stop entertainers.

Judith was entranced. She knew she was staring, and that Kelly would lecture her later, but she couldn't help herself. Coffee was brought to the music salon, and Judith had a cappuccino covered in grated chocolate.

Her eyes were drawn to the magnificent concert

grand that reminded her so much of her great-aunt's. She had the urge to crawl underneath it and just lie there, soaking in the tremendously powerful sounds it would produce.

She didn't, of course, sedately occupying the Chesterfield beside Kelly. She glanced at her friend, noting that she was wearing her I'm-about-to-be-bored expression. 'You may find you actually enjoy it,' Judith murmured. 'I think it's simply a question of being exposed to classical music. So many people in this country aren't. There's nothing highbrow about it. Much of it was written for the masses in Italy and Germany and Russia . . . pop music of the time.'

'You've said this before, but I'm not convinced,' Kelly replied, fidgeting as she was longing for a cigarette but didn't like to light up. At last she could contain herself no longer, hissing, 'I wonder if I could pop outside for a fag.'

But Damian had already taken his place on the piano stool and was flexing his hands as if loosening every joint. Then he paused, fingers poised. He started to play from memory. There was no sheet music on the stand. Judith knew he was tackling one of Franz Liszt's most difficult pieces, a dazzling show-stopper called the *Mephisto Waltz*.

He was very talented, his hands moving like lightning over the keys, his face intent, his hair tumbling about his shoulders. Liszt's contemporaries had admired him, but rumours had spread throughout his career that he was in league with Satan. This extraordinary waltz was an example of the way in which he flouted convention, for it was supposed to be a representation of the devil dancing with his concubines.

Damian's performance was electrifying, and when he had wrung the last frenzied notes from the piano, he sat there as if in a trance, his hands resting lightly on his knees. Kelly was the first to speak.

'Wicked,' she breathed. 'I could almost be converted.'

'You're clever,' Peter said, and turned to smile at Judith. 'I must admit I've not been around the classics much. The music teacher at school made it all so dull. I spent most of the lessons making darts out of paper and seeing if I could launch them without her seeing.'

Damian seemed to wake, looking around vaguely. 'Thank you,' he said. 'You're too kind.'

Judith had risen and walked to the piano, saying, 'I've never heard anyone interpret it so conclusively. It was masterly. I'm sure the composer would have approved.'

'I often wonder what those long-dead greats would think of today's instruments, and not only that, the way music is now reproduced ... CDs, videos, audio tapes, DVD. We live in a miraculous age, Judith, and have freedom of expression undreamed of by our forebears.'

He looked across at her. His eyes blazed and he still had the air of someone whose soul had been set aside while another possessed him. Could it be the ghost of Liszt himself? His questing spirit drawn towards a kindred one?

'We'd better be going,' Kelly suggested, standing up as if wanting to make her escape before Damian gave another rendition.

'Must you?' Anna asked, with a tiny pout. She looked meaningfully at Kelly, directing the question her way.

'Work in the morning,' Kelly went on, but her voice lacked conviction. 'Saturday's our busiest day.'

'You can stay here tonight. We've plenty of room,' Damian declared, in charge once more, returning from those shadowy realms where anything could happen, and probably did.

'And you, Peter?' Anna nodded encouragingly at him.

'Love to. We close on Saturdays. Are you into it, Judith?'

'OK,' she returned with a shrug, pretending to be unmoved either way, though really she was gagging for further conversation with Damian, trying to make sense of the powerful attraction that was making her forget any other man existed.

He leaned down to whisper into her hair, 'Come, my child, come with me. I can show you sights you've never even imagined, take you to places that will astound you. And when I fuck you, it'll be like no other fuck . . . not even Adam, and he's my pupil.'

She started and stared into his eyes, drowning in the depths of his inky pupils. When she looked away, she couldn't be sure if he had really said those inflammatory words, or if she'd imagined them. Now he whisked everyone off to the games room, and there they engaged in billiards. It was late, and she was more than a little tipsy by the time they were conducted upstairs and shown to their quarters.

'You'll be comfortable here,' Anna said, when she and Kelly entered a room a little way from Judith's. 'It has an en suite shower, toilet and bidet.'

'Thank you,' Kelly said, dropping her shoulder bag on the wide, mahogany bed. 'Wish I'd known we were staying, though. I haven't even brought a toothbrush or a spare pair of knickers.'

Anna walked to the chest-of-drawers and opened them one by one. 'No need to fret,' she said, and, sure enough, there was everything a guest might require, including a dozen heavenly sets of expensive under-wear. 'This, too,' Anna added, and fished out a long, black, lifelike vibrator, pressed the switch and set it humming.

She lifted her skirt and introduced the head of it to her depilated pussy. She sighed deeply and closed her eyes, running the penis-substitute over her crack, wetting it with juice, but always returning to the source of female satisfaction – her clitoris.

Kelly burned to join in. She had been right. Anna enjoyed the best of all possible worlds, an aficionado of sex in every form. Anna's eyes were narrowed with approaching ecstasy, then, 'Let me,' Kelly begged.

Anna leaned back against the wall, bracing her legs and holding her skirt high as Kelly knelt between them, focusing her attention on that pink, denuded cleft where the lips swelled and the clitoris was so large that it resembled a tiny penis. Taking the vibrator from Anna's hand, she rubbed it each side of the deep-pink nubbin, stimulating the folds. Anna raised her hands and fingered her nipples, hard as pebbles, standing out from the brown areolae.

Kelly passed the vibrator along Anna's cleft and pressed it into her slippery vulva, then, holding it steady with one hand, she began a slow, in and out movement. At the same time, she pressed the soft lips apart and ran a tender tongue-tip over the stiff, randy little organ. Anna shuddered and flicked her nipples, then rubbed and rolled them.

'Yes . . . oh, yes,' she moaned, and thrust her pelvis into Kelly's face, rocking on the dildo. Kelly could feel the vibrations, tasting Anna's sweetness, smelling her piscine scent, relishing the feel of that stiff button between her lips and under her tongue. Her own engorged clit was demanding attention.

It was some time since she had enjoyed the flesh of a woman, and now all the delights of such an encounter came rushing back. Men were fine – when one was in the mood for a hearty bonk – but women had so much more to offer a sensualist like Kelly. She knew just how she liked her own clit sucked, and performed this service for Anna. She could feel the woman's body start to twitch, and pressed hard on her clit, using a circular tonguing motion. Anna's responses were getting wilder, and Kelly shut her eyes, reliving her own sensations when on the receiving end of cunnilingus.

I hope she'll return the favour when I've brought her off, Kelly thought, and increased her efforts, but gently, knowing that if the feeling became too intense she should hold back a little, giving Anna respite by fondling the side wings, letting the clit cool down and throb for more. This was the art of love-play, this knowledge of when to act and when to pause, prolonging the lead up to bliss.

'Oh, now ... do it *now*!' Anna pleaded, her pelvis thrusting frantically.

Kelly couldn't answer, her mouth buried in Anna's crotch, but she nodded and increased the magical probing of her tongue. Anna shouted, and came in a mad rush. Kelly felt her clit throb and her cunt convulse and tighten round the fingers she had thrust inside her, the dildo discarded.

'Now you,' Anna panted, leaning against her as she recovered. 'Take off your jeans. Let me see your sweet pussy.'

Kelly slipped her feet out of her high-wedged mules, and undid her belt. The jeans were so tight that she had to wriggle to get them down. Her T-shirt was long, reaching to the apex of her thighs. It rode up as

Kelly settled herself on the bed and waited for Anna to join her. Then she closed her eyes and surrendered to the delight of being attended to by an expert. Her heart was pounding, every sense acute as Anna pushed aside the scrap of satin that formed her panties. Her breath warmed Kelly's mound, every hair on her bush standing up in response. Then there were fingers, holding her labia wings apart and an exquisite tongue performing a butterfly dance over her straining clitoris.

She came in two seconds flat.

It was too quick. She felt cheated.

'Don't worry. The night is young,' Anna said, arms around her, mouth close to hers. 'Tell me about Peter. Where does he fit into the equation?'

'He's Judith's boyfriend,' Kelly replied, winding her legs round Anna's, so that they lay pubis pressed to pubis.

'He wants to be dominated,' Anna said confidently.

'The hell he does,' Kelly answered, surprised. 'He never struck me as having sub tendencies.'

'Take my word for it. I know.' Anna untwined herself from Kelly, walked to the wardrobe and took out two leather outfits, one black and one red. 'Let's get into this dominatrix gear and pay him a visit.'

Peter had a shower and put on a pair of pyjamas that Fadil had laid out for him. They were made of silk, a far cry from the ordinary, striped, brushed-cotton ones that his mother purchased for him from Marks & Spencer's. The silk caressed his skin like intimate little fingers, and he had trouble restraining his semi-erection, which wanted to poke out through the front opening. He'd been in this state ever since he'd first seen Anna. There was something about her. He couldn't quite decide what, though the ridiculous notion popped unbidden into his head that she reminded him of his mother.

He dismissed it. Mother was your average sort of middle-aged housewife type, a widow who was devoted to her only son; a pillar of the church, organising the flower-arranging team, and an important figure in the WI. She would never, in a million years, look or act anything like Anna, though she did have that same air of confidence.

Peter wondered if it would be possible to sneak into Judith's room. He needed to relieve the pressure building up in his balls. His cock was fully erect now, curving towards his navel, and he couldn't resist stroking it. He watched himself in the dressing-table mirror, seeing those exotic, mulberry-coloured pyjamas, the front unbuttoned over his hairy chest and embryonic beer belly. He sucked it in, posing, with his hand manipulating that organ of which he was so proud. He liked its size and girth. Sometimes, he slyly compared it with other men's, when he was in a public toilet or in the shower after playing football. He had nothing to be ashamed of, and he stretched his cock. It grew larger, the shaft darkening, the helm a fiery red, dew escaping from the slit. It was meaty and he gloried in it, squeezing and pumping it, then slowing down, glancing round nervously.

He wished he were home in his own modern room where the furniture was fitted and he slept on a double futon. Mother didn't care for old-fashioned things, horrified at the idea of anything second-hand and antique contaminating her spruce three-bedroomed semi. Her house shone, the air redolent of spray polish and bleach. Still grasping his cock, he glanced round disparagingly. He supposed the stuff was valuable, but it wasn't to his taste at all. He had already decided what furniture he would choose when he and Judith were married. He'd use the same chain store as his mother, where everything from a lavatory brush to a three-piece suite could be obtained. Even better, it was possible to leave a wedding-present list there, so that those invited to the reception could order gifts and have them despatched to the happy couple.

He searched for a packet of tissues, found them and took up a position where he could watch himself come. He stroked and rubbed his penis, stretched back the foreskin and then slid it high over the mushroom-shaped helm. This was the most wonderful of games, even better than when he fucked Judith, for then he had to think about her enjoyment, when all he wanted to do was concentrate on his own. And he was always left with the feeling that she hadn't reached the peak. She never said anything, but several times after intercourse he had been aware that she was rubbing herself between the legs when she thought he was asleep. He'd not let her know, but had been aroused by that regular movement as she massaged her slit, and her deep sigh when she had brought herself off.

The memory of this made his cock jerk. He could feel the force gathering at the base of his spine and knew that he was about to spend.

'No you don't, you disgustingly vulgar boy,' said a female voice and, for a blinding instant, he thought it was his mother's.

Anna stood in the doorway, a sight to drive a monk to damnation, dressed in scarlet from head to foot. Her blonde hair was piled high, her breasts jacked up by a figure-clenching basque, her legs and lower thighs tightly enclosed in leather boots with six-inch heels.

Her pubis was naked, and even more eye-catching as it was hairless, her slit clearly defined.

Peter's cock started to droop, for though his lust increased, it was laced with guilt and terror. He'd never been caught wanking before, and didn't know whether to be ashamed or defiantly proud of his magnificent tool.

To his increased horror, he saw Kelly behind Anna. She sported a sleek black PVC catsuit, complete with gloves and stilt-heeled shoes. Though they sparred and sniped at each other on a regular basis, Peter had always wanted her, sometimes using her image as an aid to self-relief.

'Kelly, what are you doing here?' he asked, attempting to stuff his cock in the pyjama fly.

'Don't bother to put it away,' Anna answered sternly, pacing round him. 'And Kelly's with me, if it's any concern of a contemptible worm like you. I decided that you needed to be punished. And I was right. What do I find when I come in? You, playing with that filthy object. You were wanking, weren't you?'

She swished the riding crop she carried and its flat leather tip flicked across Peter's arse. It stung through the silk and he jumped, but even as he did so, he could feel his cock dribbling. 'I was ... I was ... It's the strange room, you see ... the strange situation. It makes me nervous and I do it to comfort myself,' he spluttered.

'So you jerk off like you were using a security blanket, eh?' she snarled, and brought the whip down across his thighs.

'That's right. You won't tell Judith, will you, Kelly?' he begged, rubbing his stinging flesh.

These females, in their outlandish gear, with their

103

menacing attitudes and the whips in their hands, were exciting him beyond his wildest dreams. He had never dared give credence to the fact that the thought of being tied up and abused by women turned him on. And as for that other, weird desire to wear a frock, stockings and knickers while they did it? Peter refused even to dwell on it, though it was becoming increasingly hard under these unusual circumstances.

'I may tell Judith. It depends on how you behave. Don't try to ease the blows,' Kelly sneered, unzipping her catsuit all the way down the front and standing very close to him. He could smell her spicy, pungent odour, and couldn't resist reaching out to touch the russet whorls of pussy fur adorning her mound, but was slapped smartly. 'From now on, you are under our orders. Understand?'

'Yes,' he averred, thrilled to have her shouting at him. She was magnificent. Like a goddess. He wanted to fall down and worship her. Two goddesses, and he didn't know which one he adored the most. 'Kelly, why didn't you say something before? Why didn't you tell me?'

She swished the many-thonged tawse she held in her right hand. It landed across his stomach. 'Don't be impertinent! I didn't consider you worthy. Mistress Anna is prepared to try you out.'

'Thank me for my generosity,' Anna commanded, her hands on each of his shoulders. 'Strip, worm, then kneel and lick my boots.'

Peter hesitated, but Anna glared at him until he took off his pyjama jacket. The cool air played over his skin and the wine-red discs of his nipples crimped. He loosened the knot of the cord that held the trousers up, and they dropped to the floor. He was embarrassed yet pleasantly aroused to display himself to these two beautiful women. The lads at football would never believe him were he to tell them. They were a randy crew with foul tongues, always denigrating females, though most of it was bluster as far as he could tell. But as for him? He was really, truly showing off his wares.

He thrust out his chest and strutted, but Anna caught him a savage blow across his bare rump, making him yelp. 'That's not fair!' he cried, hopping out of her reach.

'What d'you think you are? The answer to a maiden's prayer? Clean my boots, you toad. At once!'

Angered, even indignant, Peter complied, sinking down to her feet, but this raw humiliation was having a reverse effect on his cock. It was as stiff as a broom handle, bobbing in its aching need and weeping from its single eye. On his hands and knees, buttocks raised high, his brown, puckered anus was fully exposed, his balls hanging like fruit in a net. Kelly was behind him and he knew she was assessing his equipment.

From his position, face near Anna's spiked toes, Peter was given an amazing view of the length of her legs towering above him, and an uninterrupted picture of her naked, jewel-encrusted cunt. Her clit was large, the cowl pierced by a diamond. It glittered hypnotically. He would have given his eye-teeth to touch it, rub it, suck it. Would she permit him to bring her to orgasm?

'Lick my boots clean,' she grated, swiping at his back with the whip. 'I expect them as shiny as new. Even the soles, mark you. No slacking.'

Peter was no stranger to shoes, particularly those worn by women. It had been one of his chores to polish his mother's every day – winter boots, zipped and fleecy-lined; court shoes with medium heels for best; slip-ons for daily wear. Anna's leather boots were decorated with studs and had spurs fastened by straps round the ankles and under the instep. They were intriguing, awesome, so sexually stimulating that Peter was on the edge of spurting. He filled his mouth with saliva and licked every square inch, tasting the tang of the hide, the polish that dressed it, the heat of her foot inside.

As he slurped at the uppers and then the soles, he felt himself sliding into a curiously peaceful place, as if he had at last found a purpose in life. Anna's perfume, the way in which she stood, legs spread, hands on her hips, and the knowledge that Kelly hovered there, awaiting the order to use the tawse on his naked hind, seemed the most perfect thing in the world.

'Right. That's enough,' Anna barked. 'The collar, I think, Kelly.'

He was kicked to his feet and Anna took a brass-studded dog collar from Kelly and buckled it round Peter's throat. A chain dangled from it and she flicked his nipples, saying, 'These need to be pierced, then I can put rings through them and add further restraints.'

She sufficed with the one attached to the collar, stretching it down and wrapping it round Peter's massive erection. The bondage supported it, even when he dropped to his knees like a faithful pet, crawling round with Anna dragging at a leash clipped to a swivel on the choker.

His knees were sore from the carpet, his cock was painfully full, and each time he passed Kelly, she rained down blows with the leather strap that had been sliced into strips for greater punishment. Peter's rump was burning, his waist and back, too, but with each mean cut his excitement built. He lifted a hand to his cock, but Anna struck, catching him on the sensitive glans.

'Ouch! That hurt! Mind my tackle!' he shouted.

'Then don't try to jack off. I shall tell you when you may do it,' she cried, her eyes pure, glittering purple.

'Oh, please . . .'

'Mistress!'

'Please, mistress. Let me do it. I can't hold on.'

'Up,' she ordered, jerking the lead and half strangling him. 'Across that table. I can see that this vile object needs a severe welting, Mistress Kelly.'

Almost beside himself with passion, Peter spread himself over the low table. His hands were placed on the far edge, his legs kicked apart, every part of his rear vulnerable. He groaned as a double wave of agony and heated desire poured through him – Anna's riding crop and Kelly's tawse. His chest and belly were flat against the surface, but his cock brushed against the table's rim every time he scooted forward, unable to keep still under the blows.

He could feel it coming, that hot, unstoppable surge, experiencing the biggest spasm known to man or devil. He spurted jets of milky emission on to the wood and the rug beneath him.

'Dirty sod!' Anna hissed, bending over and gripping his balls. 'You realise that you're my slave now, don't you? Mine to do with as I like.'

'Yes, mistress,' he gasped.

'Then you can rim my arse and lick my clit,' she said haughtily. 'And when I've come, and it better be good, you can do the same for Mistress Kelly.'

The room was pitch dark. Judith regretted not leaving the bedside light on. But, disoriented by alcohol, she had been glad to slip out of her clothes and into the big four-poster. She'd fallen asleep straight away, but now something had awakened her.

Was it a movement? The rustle of clothing? A sigh?

She didn't know, and lay there on her back, hardly daring to breathe, straining her eyes in an effort to penetrate the gloom. 'Peter?' she whispered. 'Is that you?'

There was no answer. It could be him, she thought, though that would be rather out of character – too daring – but maybe the Rectory was weaving its spell over him as it had done her. A coil wound tight inside her, a longing for someone to make love to her as Adam had done. How marvellous it would be if he had arrived in the small hours, found out which guest room she was using and come to her in secret.

She tried this out, murmuring, 'Adam? When did you get here?', and didn't know whether to be glad or sorry when he didn't answer. It must be Kelly, she concluded, and said irritably, 'Kelly, stop messing about.'

Then she felt hands on her breasts, large hands, male hands. Shocked into immobility, she lay there, her heart beating fast. Thumbs stroked over her nipples, followed by the feel of a mouth, a tongue, the scrape of stubble. One thing was for sure: this wasn't Kelly. Then she recognised the scent of the body lotion from earlier in the evening. She could have sworn that it was Damian. But why? Why the cloak and dagger stuff?

Her vagina was slick with anticipation, his sure-fire touch on her nipples making her moan. Now she could feel the hardness of him under some sort of robe, a dressing gown perhaps; hard muscles, hard arms, hard cock. His hand went down to her pubis, lifting the hem of the nightgown Anna had supplied. She shivered at the sudden chill, then sighed as fingers parted her labial wings, found her nectar and spread it over her clitoris.

He didn't delay, keeping up a steady motion until Judith reached an explosive climax, clinging to him, her arms around his neck, wanting him, ready to accept his invasion of her body. But, to her surprise, he withdrew from her until there was no trace left of him. She reached across the bed but her groping fingers encountered nothing.

'Damian, don't go,' she begged, and pressed the lamp switch.

The room was deserted. He had come to her in the night like a phantom, and just as swiftly and silently fled away.

'We're having a bash tonight, and would love you to spend the day at the Rectory and stay for the party. Adam will be here,' Anna said over breakfast next morning.

'No can do,' Kelly said, helping herself to toast and spreading butter on it. 'There's work and I'll have to go home and get something to wear, Anna. So will Judith, won't you, Jude?'

Judith sat there looking bemused. Had something happened during the dark hours, Kelly wondered? Did she guess that Peter had been a slave? He most probably still was, for Anna was unlikely to let go. Once a sub, always a sub, she thought to herself with a secret chuckle. What a household this is, to be sure! I saw Fadil coming out of Anna's room this morning and he didn't look as if he'd been bringing her a cup of tea. More likely massaging her – she did say something about him being skilled – followed by the insertion of his extra large, circumcised member into her cunt.

'I've told you to stop worrying about clothes. It's to

be a fancy-dress party, anyway, and we've trunks full of costumes in the attic. I've already squared your absence with Adam. Oh, do say you'll stay,' Anna said silkily, and the look in her eyes spoke volumes. There was a lot of unfinished business between them, and the idea of further sex sessions made Kelly's pussy ache.

'I think that's a great idea,' Damian agreed, glancing over the top of the newspaper. 'Our parties are renowned, amongst our circle of friends.'

'I'll have to make a couple of phone calls,' Peter chipped in brightly. 'Aren't mobiles just about the best thing since sliced bread?'

'You've hit the nail right on the head, my dear chap,' Damian replied with such irony that Kelly winced. It sailed unnoticed over Peter, but Judith looked uncomfortable.

Damian's a supercilious twat, Kelly decided, but the party sounds a gas. What gives here? And how close is Adam to the almost incestuous couple, for she was convinced that they shared more than simple cousinly affection. Anna was rapacious, sadistic and insatiable. It was logical to assume that Damian was the same.

'Seems like you've talked us into it,' she said, nodding to Fadil when he hovered at her elbow with the coffee pot. 'When is Adam likely to show?'

'When he's shut the shop,' Damian answered, giving her a sardonic smile.

She had the strong feeling that he was puzzled and intrigued by her. She hadn't fallen down and worshipped him as the majority of females presumably did, and possibly some of the men. She recognised master material and it amused her to deny him, even though there hadn't been the smallest suggestion of her becoming his submissive.

She had come to the scene quite young, introduced to it by a man twice her age. He had been halfway there, an authoritative figure, one of her lecturers at university. She was a green girl, but had quickly understood the nuances of the relationship between master/mistress and slave. For her own part, she had always been brattish, learning early in life that the only way to get attention was to do something bad and get punished. A convent-school upbringing had exacerbated a tendency already ingrained. She had confused punishment with love. Later, she had discovered that she could also take the dominant role, as she had done last night with Peter.

'And will Adam be wearing masquerade costume, too?' she persisted, determined to needle Damian.

'Of course.' He lifted the paper again, putting a screen between them.

After breakfast, he went off for a fencing bout with his trainer, and Anna took Kelly, Judith and Peter upstairs to the attic.

It had once been the servants' bedroom, in the days when the manse had been the centre of village life, almost as much as the public house. But for years it had been used for storage. The light came from cobweb-draped windows, picking out the lumber of former generations and items of furniture or ornaments which might come in handy one day, or were too valuable to be donated to charity. There were children's toys from the early twentieth century that would have fetched a bomb at auction: a rocking horse, a doll's house, a coach-built doll's pram whose occupant was china-headed and must have been over a hundred years old.

Were the Cresswells so rich that they didn't bother to root through their possessions and cull a few? Kelly wondered, her predator's eye evaluating the contents. They professed to know about antiques, didn't they? It couldn't be that they were keeping these relics for sentimental reasons. There wasn't an ounce of sentimentality in either of them, as far as she could ascertain. Beside which, they'd only been there a short while, or so they said. It wasn't as if it was a family home. Perhaps the toys and clothes had been part and parcel of the purchase, left by former occupants? Every piece of information she gleaned about the Cresswells made her all the more curious.

Anna went straight to a cabin trunk half covered by a tattered cashmere shawl. She pushed it aside and flung back the lid. There was the throat-catching smell of mothballs, and a sunbeam flashed off diamanté trimmings, paste buckles, tarnished tinsel, jet, velvet and ruffles and splendid red military jackets.

There was a wardrobe behind the trunk and this held further costumes, crinolines and bustles, corsets and pantaloons, and old-style frock coats. 'Isn't this wicked?' Anna cried gleefully, robbing hangers and snatching up accessories. 'Let's have fun.'

Pictures flashed across Kelly's mind. The Victorian photographs in all their outrageous, blatant eroticism. The clothes were of that period, surely? The feminine garments bore an aura of wantonness: low necklines, pinched in waists, frilly knickers with an open crotch, fans to flirt with, button boots and black stockings to drive men wild.

And those stuffy, ever-so-respectable men's clothes, with starched collars and shirt fronts and, no doubt, equally stiff dicks, hidden behind a show of respectability. Scratch the surface, however, and a bubbling cauldron of lust was revealed.

'Come on. Dress up,' Anna insisted, already stripping off her wide-legged pants and silk sweater, naked beneath. She held out a pair of purple satin corsets and presented her shapely back to Kelly. 'Lace me up as tight as you can. I'll hang on to this beam so you can get a purchase. That's it! Ooh, lovely! I can feel the restriction. It's like all my blood is concentrated round my fanny.'

Kelly heaved on the lacing, hoping age wouldn't let it down, but it seemed as strong as the day it was made. Anna's waist shrank and, in front, her breasts rose up, the skin flushed, the pointed teats poking over the yellowing lace. Anna admired herself in a fly-spotted cheval mirror on a cracked mahogany stand. Kelly thought she looked outstandingly tarty, a sixpenny whore who roved the backstreet pubs of Dickensian London in search of punters. The image sent a flood of longing through her cunt, and her panties dampened under her jeans.

If she'd lived in the days of daguerreotypes, Anna would have posed for those earthy photos. Now Kelly saw her as a French harlot, an artist's model, perhaps, who had found working for photographers better paid and not so taxing. Anna stepped into a pair of cambric drawers that opened all the way round the gusset, and found the right stockings, black and upheld by garters, and managed to squeeze her feet into ankle boots, using a button hook to fasten them.

'Wow!' Peter was impressed. 'What gear! I've always wanted ... had this idea, you know ... of dressing in that stuff.'

I was bang on, Kelly thought, satisfied. He's a closet transvestite.

Chapter 6

JUDITH COULDN'T TAKE IN what was happening. Peter, wanting to dress as a girl? Peter, the leading light of the football team, the public bar swaggerer, Mr Macho himself, standing there with a bustle in his hand, his cock erect with excitement. What was going on?

She was suddenly conscious that Kelly and Anna knew more about him than she did. What had happened between them last night, while an incubus was seducing her? Waking to find herself sticky between the legs, she had succeeded in composing a scenario in which her nocturnal visitor hadn't been human. It was too much to hope that it had been Damian, especially as he'd ignored her at breakfast. So far she'd had no chance to talk it over with Kelly.

She wanted to leave the Rectory, but at the same time wanted to stay. Adam was expected and Damian had promised her pleasure, unless that, too, had been in her imagination.

But Peter was real enough, undoing his trainers and taking off his jeans and boxer shorts and hauling his borrowed sweatshirt over his head. He retained his socks, which Judith thought made him look utterly ridiculous. Kelly and Anna found a large, pink, whale-boned corset, folded it round him from chest to hipbone and strained at the laces. His breath rushed out, his waist went in and his cock stood up before him like a lance. He was obviously hugely turned on.

'Now the petticoat,' Anna said, and he clambered into it, his erection tenting the material as she adjusted the waistband. 'I don't think there's a bodice big enough, but try this feather boa.'

He wrapped it round his shoulders and stared at himself, a satisfied smirk on his face. A wet spot appeared on the petticoat covering his rod. Anna smiled and gripped it through the cloth. Peter moaned and thrust into her hand.

'Here, Judith. Try this on,' urged Kelly, and placed a bundle into Judith's arms. She was already half naked, and had squirmed into a pair of cream linen stays a size too small for her.

Judith shook out the oyster satin ball-gown and its accompanying underwear. It breathed an aroma of faded flowers, lavender water and romantic love. Had a young girl worn this, perhaps at her first grown-up occasion? Had there been a dashing young man who had urged her to add his name to her dance-card? She held the dress up against herself and looked in the mirror.

Nothing could have been more innocent. Not so the scene being enacted behind her.

'I'm going to call you Fifi,' Anna said to Peter, bossily. 'You'll be my maid for the night. Now then, slag, what have you been up to? Letting men fuck your arse without my permission? This deserves severe chastisement. Don't you agree, Mistress Kelly? How about you, Mistress Judith?'

Judith assumed this to be a rather sick joke, but

115

didn't know what to say. She prevaricated with a, 'Whatever you think best, Anna.'

Kelly seemed really into it. She had changed into a black riding habit, with a jacket cut like a man's and a carelessly tied jabot edging the shirt that was open to the waist. A low-crowned topper concealed her hair, complete with a snood and a black veil. She wore riding boots and no knickers, the skirt slit to the waist at one side. It was designed to wrap round over narrow trousers, but Kelly scorned this idea, displaying her foxy bush. She strutted up and down, stirring the dust balls on the bare floorboards, and swishing her crop as she went, sometimes smacking it against her thigh.

Judith gulped, taken off guard by the stab of longing that shot through her. Kelly looked amazing, slim and keen-hipped as a boy. She exuded bravura, taking every situation in her stride. And she's my friend, Judith thought with a glow of pride. I hope she doesn't forget that and become too engrossed with Anna.

Unlike a professional drag queen, Peter would never be mistaken for anything other than a man. He was awkward, his feet and hands too big, his shoulders too broad and his posterior too flat. He seemed ignorant of this, enamoured of himself, preening in the mirror and adjusting a curly auburn wig that he had placed over his own short, fair hair.

'I need make-up,' he complained pettishly, straightening his spine. He ran his hands down his torso to his pinched-in waist. His chest swelled above it, coated with brownish fuzz. 'I can't go to the party looking a frump.'

'You will if I tell you,' Anna stated, and signalled to Kelly. 'Fifi's getting too uppity, Mistress Kelly. Use your crop on her big, fat arse.'

Peter immediately bent over and clasped his ankles, his bottom raised. Anna flung up his petticoat and smothered his head in the folds. Judith was embarrassed to see his nakedness, the ludicrous socks, the stout thighs, the male buttocks, and the amber crack between. Then, with a swish, Kelly lifted her arm and brought the crop down viciously. It met his skin with a thwack. He bucked and gave a muffled cry.

'Shut up and take your punishment,' Anna commanded, and reached below him, finding his penis and holding it in her fist, using a milking motion.

'Oh, oh . . . bring me off, mistress,' he pleaded, gripping his ankles tightly.

'No,' Anna said decisively. 'You don't deserve it. Here, do this.'

She slithered under him, flat on her back, and pushed her pussy into his face. Her hands were holding back the vertical slit in the drawers, baring her fissure to his mouth. He slurped at her and Kelly continued to beat him. Judith didn't know where to look. She was disgusted, yet so aroused that her panties were soaking. She couldn't resist lifting her dress and pushing her fragile briefs aside, finding her greedy nubbin, heat pulsing through it.

'That's right, Judith. Go for it,' Kelly encouraged, and Judith obeyed her, too far along the line to stop. She fucked herself with her hand at a furious pace and came with a gasp.

She was ahead of Anna, returning to her senses to see her lifting her hips from the floor and grinding her pubis into Peter's face, crying out as her crisis shook her. Kelly was using the crop as a dildo, wetting the handle at her vulva before trailing it over her cleft, twirling it round her clit, and then pushing it inside her, inch by inch. Her catsuit was fully unzipped, giving easy access to her cunt and arsehole. As she moved the crop delicately in and out, the fingers of her right hand massaged her clit. Standing with legs open, she threw back her head, face contorted as she reached her own apogee.

'That will do as a starter,' Anna said, prone beneath Peter.

'Can I come now, mistress?' he begged.

'You may. We shall watch. Gather round, girls,' she said, and pushed him off.

He sank back on his haunches, his balls tight, his iron-hard cock clenched in his hand. The women's clothes he wore looked incongruous against these very male organs, but the obscene, freaky nature of this aberration was visually exciting. Judith couldn't stop staring at him, and at what he was doing to himself. Anna stood on one side of her and Kelly the other, both women watching Peter intently, waiting breathlessly for that second when he would shoot his semen.

Groaning as he pumped his cock, Peter seemed unaware of them, or if he was aware, then uncaring. Judith found it almost impossible to come to terms with the transformation that had occurred within him. Here was a libidinous creature, a satyr in corsets, petticoat and an absurd ginger wig. But he was giving her a glimpse of his own private heaven. She'd never watched a man wanking before and her loins ached for another orgasm followed by deep, hard penetration by a large cock.

Peter sighed and shuddered, his overcharged tool giving vent to rapid-fire spurts, the thick creamy goo landing on his hand.

'Show's over,' Anna announced, and turned her attention back to the clothes. 'There's a load to choose from. We'd better get down to it. The guests will start arriving mid-afternoon.'

'You've done well,' Damian said, as he and Adam watched the performance in the attic through a monitor. He had excused himself with talk of a fencing lesson, but in reality he had been indulging in a spot of voyeurism. 'The girls are lovely,' he went on, 'especially the little innocent, Judith. And the young man is a bonus. Anna's very pleased with you. No doubt she'll reward you in her own, inimitable way.'

'I don't expect a reward,' Adam expostulated. 'I'm her slave. Yours, too.'

He had been there at breakfast time, hidden in Damian's den where the whole interior of the house could be observed through a bank of screens; the summerhouse and gardens as well. When Damian had summoned him, he had called on a colleague to mind the shop and ridden to the Rectory on his classic motorcycle. He was wearing clothes of the era: gauntlets, a leather jacket, cord breeches tucked into heavyweight boots, and a Biggles flying helmet complete with goggles. He was ready for the fancy-dress party, masquerading as an ace of the early racing circuits.

'I want to take them to Paris and then on to the château,' Damian said, and he signalled for Adam to move closer. 'You'll be able to manage without them?'

'I managed before, don't forget, though Kelly is more than just useful. She's making a fine job of my filing system and website.'

'But you obtained them for me, didn't you?' Damian reminded him.

'Well, yes . . . in part, but I could do with their assistance.'

'With any luck, we'll kill two birds with one stone. But I must have them with me when I go abroad. Say, at the end of next week? I'm sure you can cope for a few days.'

Damian slumped in a large armchair. He had rewound the video recording he had made of the attic antics. Now he was looking directly at the screen where Judith was masturbating as she watched Kelly belting Peter's rump.

'You're seeing Philippe Laveau?' Adam asked, accepting Damian's high-handed instructions, as he always did. He would have liked to go with them, but had obviously played his part for the time being.

'Yes. He's entertaining in his Paris house. It will be interesting to observe Judith's reaction. I'm negotiating with him for a photograph attributed to Paul Antoine.'

'The man who liked to concentrate on full, head-on shots of women's cunts, in 1850 or thereabouts?'

'That's him. Laveau is considering selling one from his collection.'

'He'll be asking a fortune.'

'He will, but if I take over a little sweetener, then he may be prepared to drop the price,' Damian reflected, fondling his exposed cock and staring at Judith's image as she reached her climax.

'He's depraved,' Adam said.

Damian shrugged and replied, 'That's a matter of opinion and depends on one's viewpoint at any given time.'

Adam looked down at him admiringly. Damian was such a handsome man, with his beautiful black hair and tiger's eyes. Multi-talented, he could seduce with music, sweep one away with the breadth of his intellect, and lure one to hell with his sensuality. And now

Adam was gazing, fascinated, at the man's phallus. Even this managed to look elegant. It was long and thick, the swarthy skin of the shaft knotted with veins, the glans red and moist. Adam was almost as familiar with it as he was his own. He was equally familiar with Anna's beautiful, orchid-shaped cunt, with the rosy pistil at its crown, that fat little knob which responded frantically to lips, fingers or tongue.

I suppose some people might call me their dogs-body, always running around on errands for them, but I like it, hunger for their approval, consider myself blessed when they let me orgasm in their sight, he thought. He crouched lower, smelling Damian's essential odour, yearning to sip his nectar that tasted not unlike Anna's.

'No,' Damian said, guessing his intent. His hand left his cock and trailed jism across Adam's cheek. 'Not now. I'm saving myself for tonight. Little Miss Shaw needs training. She has an untried arse and a barely used pussy. I'm looking forward to exploring both.'

'I tied her, spanked her, went down on her,' Adam said, aware of the heat gathering in his balls, inspired by memories of Judith and the presence of his master.

'So you told me. It is now my privilege to further her education.'

Despite Judith's protestations, Kelly and Anna had decided that she must be dressed as an ingénue. No burlesque artiste, or flirtatious lady, or even a street-walker. Though the theme of the party was *The Secret Victorians*, she had to appear in an ankle-length flounced skirt, a round-necked bodice and puff sleeves. Under this she wore frilled pantalets, which consisted of two quite separate legs, sewn on to a waistband. They finished just below the knee, were draughty, and easily exposed the wearer's private parts. Red and white striped stockings and flat-heeled black pumps, à la Alice in Wonderland, completed her costume.

'I feel a right prat in this,' she complained, gazing in the mirror while Kelly fixed a blue ribbon in her hair.

'Don't freak. You look wicked. Damian will go crazy over you. Now, sit still, we need a touch of blusher, a smidgen of eye-shadow and mascara and a cupid's bow mouth.'

'But you and Anna have chosen revealing costumes. I want to wear one like yours, Kelly. That riding habit is so suggestive.'

'And needs to be worn by someone who can handle it and knows how to use a whip. Sit still!' Kelly gave her a poke.

'And even Peter looks the part in that corset and bustle.'

'Anna and I spent a long time shaving his chest and making him up. He's almost a girl now. We even found a pair of size ten shoes, though that was hard. Women in the olden days had much smaller hands and feet than now, but there were some at the bottom of the trunk. Maybe one of the vicars was into cross-dressing. What about you and him, anyway? Is it on or off?'

'That's dead in the water. Has been for some time,' Judith said, and felt sad. 'I never knew him all that well, it seems. What on earth's got into him?'

'He's just being himself. Didn't you suspect he had wacky fantasies?'

'No. I bet you think I'm really stupid.'

'Not at all. Just naïve. The Rectory will soon sort you out. Don't be surprised by anything you see tonight, and come and find me if things get a bit too rough. I don't think they will. Damian will look after you.'

'Will he give me a safe word, like Adam did?' Judith was acutely nervous.

'It depends what happens. Don't worry. Just enjoy yourself. This is a lot more fun than labouring over a hot computer.'

All afternoon, Judith had been aware of cars drawing up outside. Peering from her window, she saw that the semi-circular drive was gradually filling up with Jaguars, Rovers, BMWs and the occasional Porsche. Whoever the Cresswells' friends were, they were moneyed and probably influential, maybe even titled. And was Adam here yet? Her heart skipped a beat and her nipples contracted under the corset she wore beneath her dress.

He was the first person she saw when she came down the staircase into the hall. He held out his hands and clasped hers warmly, saying, 'Judith, how lovely you look.'

'Thank you,' she replied, wishing she was wearing something more sophisticated and risqué. Then, looking around her, she realised that Kelly's choice had been just right.

There were enough ladies in leather or satin bustiers, and a plethora of suspenders framing bare or hairy mounds, and crinoline cages uncovered by skirts, that swayed willy-nilly, exposing both cunts and buttocks. Their escorts were more conservatively attired in old-style evening suits, tailcoats, bow ties, and full army officer regalia, complete with medals and dress-swords.

Fadil and Prunella had cast off any pretence of modesty. He was naked, apart from a tiny jock strap that barely contained his bulging genitals. His body was superbly proportioned, the brown skin oiled, a white turban wound round his head. His nipples were pierced, as was his navel, and he paced among the crowd, organising the caterers, but available at all times if someone, male or female, wanted to feel his package or slip a finger into the crack of his tight-muscled buttocks.

Prunella was equally obliging, her skirt raised high at the back, her black stockings upheld by garters and falling short of her plump white thighs, her bottom cheeks criss-crossed with stripes from a recent caning, her minge coated in crisp dark hair. Her bodice was slit over each opulent breast and her nipples poked out like two cherries, inviting and delectable. She sashayed round the room on her high heels, pausing whenever a guest chose to finger her.

'How are you enjoying your stay?' Adam asked, and Judith thrilled at the sound of his voice, yet not as much as she would have done had she not met Damian.

'It's, ah . . . unusual,' she managed to get out. 'I've never met people like the Cresswells.'

'Unique, aren't they?' he agreed and took two glasses of white wine from a tray proffered by a waiter.

At first glance the waiter seemed ordinary enough, but when Judith looked more closely, she saw that his cock was poking out through a gap in his black trousers where a fly fastening should have been. It was erect, and his encouraging smile indicated that he'd have no objection if she wanted to touch it. Like Alice herself, she wanted to murmur, 'Curiouser and curiouser.' At any moment, she expected to see the Cheshire Cat's grin materialise and float over the crowd.

Adam escorted her to the dining room where a cold

collation was laid out. The food was lavish: salmon, caviar, slices of wafer-thin ham, rounds of cold beef, mountains of fruit, ice-cream, and an abundance of champagne. Damian didn't stint himself, or those he entertained. The setting was impressive, glittering with mirrors and gilt, garlanded with flowers, the walls hung with blow-ups of grainy brown and cream photographs like the ones she had seen in Adam's storeroom. Life-size, they seemed even more explicit: big cocks, enlarged clits, voluptuous breasts and swollen testicles. And the women were wearing those demure, it-isn't-really-me-doing-this expressions which made the images all the more arousing.

The guests walked around drinking champagne, admiring the photos and the various costumes. Music drifted from tall, thin speakers placed at the correct angle. Judith recognised waltzes in keeping with the party's theme. They set her hips swaying and her feet moving.

Damian had artfully arranged a series of tableaux below the blow-ups. There, living models posed, in twos or threes or even fours, immovable as statues, their attire and exposed genitalia an exact replica of the scenes on the walls. How hard it must be to stay still with a man's cock at your entrance, or your finger poised over your clit, staring at the observer with a glassy eye and a frozen smile, Judith thought.

Anna beckoned to Adam and he muttered an excuse and went to her. 'What is it about that woman that makes men go running when she crooks her little finger?' she said crossly to Peter, who was at the table, piling his plate with delicacies. 'And you are no better.'

'Look here, Judith, let me explain,' he spluttered, but wasn't really attending to what she had said, his eyes darting about as he sought out Kelly or waited for a command from Anna.

'Don't bother,' Judith snapped and left him standing.

A stage had been set up at one end of the music salon. It was equipped with a red curtain and foot-lights. Chairs had been arranged facing it and many of these were already occupied. Judith stood at the back as more and more people crowded in. A bald-headed man in a dress-suit was at the piano, ready to commence.

Anna came in with Adam, Peter mincing behind her carrying her flogger. She seated herself on a throne-like chair and clapped her hands. Fadil appeared and she said, 'Let the show begin.'

The pianist struck up and the curtain swished back. To Offenbach's music, a troupe of dancers entered from the wings and, with raucous whoops, flung themselves into the can-can. Dressed like tarts from the dives frequented by Toulouse-Lautrec, they were wearing low-cut bodices, tight velvet corsets and no knickers. As they kicked high, holding up their flounced skirts, so the audience roared their approval at the nudity of their bellies, thighs and sex. They roared even more when it became apparent that two of the most flamboyant dancers were men. They whirled, shrieked, did cart-wheels and the splits, and finished their brazen performance by facing away from the spectators, bending over, whipping up their skirts and displaying their naked bottoms.

The spectators in the front row leaped the shallow steps and landed on the stage, eager to handle the dancers.

'Sirs, ladies, please. Control yourself. You must wait your turn,' Fadil remonstrated, a rather flustered

126

Master of Ceremonies. 'Form an orderly queue. That's right, off the stage and down to your right. There are six young dancers ready to pleasure you. There will be a short intermission while we prepare for the next act, when Madame Mimi is going to delight you with a fan dance, "fan" being the operative word. We shall follow this with a Slave Auction in New Orleans.'

'Isn't this a gas?' Kelly remarked, coming to rest by Judith. 'I've never been so thoroughly felt in all my life. They're even worse than Alden's road crew, and they're randy as billy-goats. I've been propositioned right, left and centre.'

'Where's Damian?' Judith asked crisply. She'd not seen him all evening.

'You really want to know, kiddo?' Kelly said slowly. 'On your head be it. Come this way.'

The party hadn't yet degenerated into an orgy, but as Kelly led Judith to the back of the house, they peeped into discreet, shadowy nooks and alcoves where couples were slaking appetites aroused by Damian's tableaux. Judith saw men mounting men, and women lying on divans in the sixty-nine position, faces buried between one another's thighs, and heterosexuals engaged in straight copulation. In the conservatory, swimmers were enjoying the warm pool. The ladies' bathing costumes modestly covered them from neck to ankle, but the wet wool clung to their curves, leaving little to the imagination. And the men wore nothing at all. Judith had never seen so many balls, ripe as plums or wizened like prunes, and cocks long and thick or thin and weedy, ready to enter the first orifice that came into view.

'I'm becoming blasé,' she wailed, clutching at Kelly's sleeve. 'How awful to have such a surfeit of sex that you become indifferent to it.'

'That'll be the day,' Kelly said with a throaty chuckle.

'Where are we going?' Judith asked, anxious as Kelly led her through the backstairs hall, and paused before a door.

'To heaven,' Kelly replied, and pushed it open.

Darkness met the eye, then a faint reddish glow. Stone steps led downwards into the bowels of the house.

'Are these cellars?' Judith paused on the top step before venturing further.

'Not any more,' Kelly said, excitement making her voice quiver.

'Then what?'

'You'll see.'

The stairs were steep, but the air was humid. Somehow this place was connected with the boiler that fired the hot water system. Judith could feel its glow, hear its faint hums and creaks. Such normal sounds steadied her. There was nothing sinister about it. She strode out boldly, keeping up with Kelly who was forging ahead.

Now she could hear voices, and other noises, too. The snap of leather, the clink of metal on metal, a woman weeping, her voice high and anguished. Judith's confidence melted like snow in sunlight. She stopped dead in her tracks. 'Take me back,' she said.

'No. Master's orders that you're brought here,' Kelly said with a shake of her head.

'What master? Don't talk crap.' Judith spoke angrily because she was so frightened.

'You're an initiate. Can't get out of it. I'll see you're all right.'

Judith turned to run, but Kelly stopped her. 'Let me go,' Judith pleaded.

'It's OK. Nothing to worry about. You'll enjoy it. Trust me.'

In that dimly lit underground passage, facing the unknown, Judith doubted Kelly for the first time ever. Kelly was a maverick, always had been and always would be. Why should she remain loyal to someone like herself, if others, stronger and more alluring, put temptation in her way?

Feeling Judith trembling, Kelly hugged her and went on, 'Nothing bad is going to happen. Far from it. They want to take us to Paris. Isn't that something? All expenses paid.'

'Why?' Judith was still plagued by the unease that refused to be shaken off.

'They need us. We have skills they want. That's what Anna told me.'

'Anna? I wouldn't trust her further than I could fling her.'

Judith realised that while they had been talking, Kelly had inched forward. Now they had reached a door at the end of the passage. The sounds were coming from behind it. Kelly knocked twice and the door swung open, then sighed shut again behind them. With her heart beating like a long-distance runner's, Judith stepped into the room beyond. It was painted scarlet from skirting to ceiling, and the only light came from tall, floor-standing girandoles, whose iron branches bore nests of candles. Ahead lay another door, draped in sable velvet.

Kelly drew the hangings aside. The sounds from within ceased abruptly. Judith hesitated before crossing the threshold, staring into a vaulted chamber that blazed with candles in elaborate holders and flares stuck in brackets along the stone walls. Incense perfumed the air on spirals of smoke billowing from the nostrils of bronze dragons. The room was crowded, but Judith had eyes for one person only.

Damian was looking straight at her.

He was wearing a priest's long purple cassock and standing near a crosspiece to which a naked woman was bound, her cheek pressed to the upright post. Her back and buttocks were laddered with stripes, forming a regular pattern. Damian was caressing the length of supple black hide that coiled round his hand, the plaited leather shank swinging. The woman's arms were stretched above her head, her wrists tied to a ring at the top of the cross. Her ankles were roped to a rung at the base. A wooden spreader was fixed between her thighs, forcing them wide open. Her face was turned to Damian, her silver blonde hair cascading over her shoulders.

'Master, don't stop. Take me. Own me. I'm unworthy, but give me relief,' she begged, and her tears trickled down, disappearing into the lines of her throat and the divide of her large breasts.

'Be silent, bitch,' he growled, and his select coterie, sprawling on divans in a circle round the whipping-post, laughed their approval.

These were intimates, fellow hedonists of both sexes. Though costumed for this fetish event, the candle flames danced over jewels and orders, and drew sparks from the choke chains some of them had elected to wear in their roles as subs. Several women were discussing the girl on the cross, their gestures indicating that they wanted to flog her, but dared not unless instructed by the master.

Wine and canapés were served by female slaves. They wore nothing, apart from high-heeled shoes, scarlet stockings and red half-masks. Judith wanted to turn tail and run, yet her insides were churning with excitement and her clit throbbed demandingly.

'Come to me, Judith,' Damian said, and beckoned to her.

She obeyed, walking slowly over the flagstones like someone in a trance, and not pausing until she was at his side. He touched her lightly with the whip, but the contact fired through her. 'What do you want with me?' she whispered, looking up into his amber eyes.

'Kneel, child, and confess your sins,' he said, and the illusion was nearly complete. He could have been the reincarnation of a churchman who had once resided at the Rectory.

'I can't,' she murmured. 'Not in front of everyone.'

'Then you must be punished for disobedience,' he answered, regretful but stern. He snapped his fingers and two slaves crawled towards him on their hands and knees. 'Get up. Undress this rebellious girl. I want her stripped to her pantaloons.'

Judith gave Kelly an imploring glance, but she did nothing. It was as if everyone there was mesmerised by Damian, waiting breathlessly to see what he would do next. She felt nimble fingers on her back as they worked to free her bodice and remove it. Bare arms, bare shoulders, and further nudity as her chemise was taken off and then the corset.

Damian came to her, his lips curved sensuously as his hands roved over her breasts, fingers stroking her nipples. The ache within her made her clit peak. His eyes were hot, his penis hard with desire, forming a lump behind the cassock. 'You're beautiful,' he murmured, and his words stirred her like wine and fire.

Kelly had said she didn't believe in love, but Judith feared it was love she felt; or if not, enough passion to last her a lifetime. 'Thank you,' she managed to croak, her cunt turning to liquid.

'You're thanking me and you don't yet know what I'm going to do to you?' he said, and there was a trace of sardonic mirth on his face.

'I trust you,' she lied, shaking in case he was a mind-reader, too.

'That's a foolish thing to do. You think I know what's best for you?'

'I hope so.'

His hands left her breasts and he reached down between their bodies and pushed aside the legs of the pantalets, seeking out her pussy. She jumped and his hold on her tightened, pinching her mound, his middle finger crooked as he palpated her clit. She was being enticed and tempted, lost in erotic sensations. There was the taste of danger on her lips. Trembling at her own daring she let her hand coast up and down the length of his cock. She could feel its heat through the purple cloth. He grunted under his breath, and pulled away.

'You have an arse that begs to be abused,' he said. 'You dream of falling in love, but there are other pleasures to be enjoyed, without the emotional trauma. I'm about to take you on a journey, but I'm not forcing you to come and we can stop any time you like. Are you ready to be chastised for your misdemeanours?'

'Yes,' she mumbled, thinking: I must be barking mad!

She was conducted to a contraption that looked like a vaulting horse. It was waist high, and padded. It had strategically placed rings, and her heart sank as their possible uses sprang to mind.

Damian lifted her so that she lay across the centre of the bench, her head hanging down on one side, her legs on the other, with her bottom raised high in between. Her wrists were gripped, and metal, fur-lined cuffs buckled round each one. These in turn were fastened to rings. Her legs, in those revealing pantalets, were manacled and attached to further rings. She was as helpless as a stranded fish.

She waited. It seemed that the chamber had dropped into an abyss of silence and anticipation. It hung there like a protracted scream and the sweat dripped from her nipples, soaking into the padding that cushioned her. She vividly recalled the time when Adam had spanked her, and the ferocious climax that had followed. She was quivering with need, praying that Damian would do more than just restrain her. She wanted to know him, to explore his mind, his body, and his very soul. No matter what it cost her in anguish, she'd never be satisfied with less.

She moaned when she felt his fingers on her swollen mound, tracing the avenue downwards and finding her pulsing hot clitoris. His touch was light, soothing, but desperately arousing. The few almost playful slaps that followed his frottage simply aroused her more. She could feel her orgasm about to explode, but then he stopped. Tears blurred her sight. He had taken her to the edge but hadn't allowed her to climax. It was as if he didn't consider her worthy. If she suffered and took it well, then he might show mercy. It was dependent on his whim whether or not he decided that he wanted to watch her come.

His warmth left her and he backed away. Suddenly the whip sang and pain seared through her. The force and agony of it took her breath away. She jolted against her bonds but was too shocked to scream. The second blow released this pent-up noise and she howled her anguish. His hand was on her, stroking the weals, dipping into her bottom crack, finding her pursed pussy and its copious wetness and spreading this to her clit. He frigged her, then moved back and lashed her again. He repeated this several times and, each time, she was brought closer and closer to ecstasy.

The pain no longer mattered. She was drifting, her mind blank, sensations piling on one another, the agony, the fear, the smell of her own sweat and juices, the smell of his. She lost count of the number of times the whip slashed her, lost the awareness that they were being watched and that this scenario was exciting the spectators into frenzied sexual activity.

Then, just as suddenly, Damian undid the manacles and lifted her from the horse. She almost fell, and he caught her in his arms. She felt herself being carried easily in strong male arms, and then laid down on something soft and silky. She opened her eyes and looked up into the fiery red and sombre black drapes of a divan set in a velvet-lined alcove. Two tall candles burned each side of the bedhead, and a curtain part-shielded this bower for lusty lovers.

'Drink. It will help the pain and bring you to bliss,' Damian ordered, and brought a gold chalice to her lips. The wine was strong with a bitter aftertaste.

'Drugging me now, are you?' she managed to gasp, though only half believing he would stoop so low.

'No. I've never found that necessary, my dear,' he said darkly, and unbuttoned his cassock. He wore nothing underneath it.

His body was overpoweringly virile. He looked much larger when naked. He was muscle-packed – limbs, body, all perfectly tuned and in fine fettle. He was hirsute, furry across chest, arms, legs and belly, his penis thrusting upwards from the thicket of black hair at his groin. It was awesome, long in the shaft and with a bulbous head denuded of foreskin. Judith doubted that she would be able to take it all, but she wanted to try, most desperately.

He applied balm to her stripes, his hands as gentle as a woman's, and then went lower, going between her legs and working it into her labia and vulva and that perfect little nodule wherein lay her greatest pleasure. She gave a long ululating cry as her orgasm peaked and burst and shattered, sending violent shockwaves through every part of her body.

He gentled her, bringing her down like a loving trainer with a mare, stopping the animal from spooking. Then, with a mercurial change of mood, he pushed her back and knelt between her legs, holding his cock in one hand and guiding it into her wet channel. It entered her inch by inch, and the feeling was divine, her internal muscles stretching to accommodate him, his helm nudging against her cervix.

He began to move in a steady rhythm, and she went with it, welcoming the in and out motion of that amazingly large cock. Even in her highly-strung state, she was aware that it was latex caressing her, not the skin of his penis. Somehow, she didn't know when, he had taken care to protect them both. Perhaps he had arrived at the party already rubber-wrapped, knowing that his prick would come into its own during the proceedings. Such a calculating action was rather off-putting. Did he do everything according to plan?

She tightened her legs round his waist, hearing the murmurs of the guests, most of whom were watching them. She didn't care. Mrs Tanner could have stalked into the vault and Judith wouldn't have given a damn. All that mattered was Damian and the hardness of his penis and the way his balls tapped against her perineum. She pumped upwards with her hips, urging him on. Her hands rubbed up and down his arms and clasped him round the neck. She had never known such pleasure, wanting him to go deeper and harder, sure that he was about to spurt.

He didn't. Instead, he withdrew, and rolled her over, his hands under her pelvis, raising her bottom towards him. He wetted his fingers in her love juice and smeared it up her crack and into her tight anal ring. Judith wriggled, disappointed, yet feeling the start of a strange heat in her private hole. His groin was against her buttocks. She sensed his breath fluttering across her back. He reached round and cupped her mound in his hand, his fingers entering the soft wet folds of her labia and dipping into her opening. She heard the slippery sound as he withdrew them, and felt the alarming invasion as he wormed a finger into her back passage. It hurt, but she couldn't stop rocking against him, feeling the warmth of him and the pulse of his cock as it pressed like a steel bar into her crack.

His finger was lodged firmly inside her, and he moved it in and out, then added a second and a third. Now she felt painfully stretched, frightened of what lay ahead, yet dying to try it. But, 'No ... no,' she panted as his fingers left her, to be replaced by the hard, rounded snout of his prick. It was painful and she couldn't stand it, crying out.

'Relax,' he said, his breath brushing her ear. 'That's it. Let your sphincter go. Now, isn't that better? Good girl. Good little slave. Nice and easy. That's right.'

She felt raw inside, penetrated by that monstrous thing that hurt yet stimulated. Damian kept his finger on her pussy, rubbing her clit as he entered her arse steadily and without pausing, until he was fully inside her.

'Oh my God!' she squealed, trying to fight him, but feeling a strange, perverted pleasure as he ground into her.

She was terrified that he'd damage her, yet every second found her more willing. He rubbed her clit and her struggles gave way to passion. She could feel him fused to her body, and then he was losing control, riding her, chasing his orgasm. Agonised, she wriggled like an eel on that solid flesh, wanting to push him out, wanting to suck him deep inside her and keep him there for ever. He dragged himself free of her, ripped off the condom and came all over her buttocks, his seed warm and sticky on her flesh.

Judith collapsed, her rectum burning, every tender membrane within her holding its own fiery sting. He moved away from the divan, leaving her there like a discarded toy, and she heard him say to Anna who had appeared in the alcove, 'Work on her for me. Her arse is far too tight. I want her submissive and open next time I bugger her. Use butt-plugs or Ben-wa balls. I don't mind which. But do it.'

Chapter 7

JUDITH WOKE TO FIND herself in her own room. A tap on the door had disturbed her. Anna entered, followed by Prunella carrying a breakfast tray.

'Good morning, pet,' Anna carolled, and the maid put the tray down on the bedside table.

'Hello,' Judith said, rubbing her eyes. 'What time is it? Seems like I've been asleep for hours.'

'Nine o'clock. Most of the guests have gone, and I propose that you start the day with a long soak in the bath, followed by a massage. Pru and I are all set to pamper you. OK?'

'Where's Kelly?' Judith asked, sitting up and wincing at the soreness of her derrière. With the pain came a resurgence of memory. It made her flush all over. Damian, whipping her in front of an audience, then copulating with her – going further than normal intercourse – arse-fucking her!

'She'll be along soon. She's going to help us.'

'To do what? I'm perfectly capable of washing myself,' Judith muttered indignantly, pushing aside the bowl of cereal, the triangles of buttered toast, and the coffee. She took a sip of orange juice and then set the tray to one side.

'Darling, we're going to give you the works,' Anna said, with a captivating smile. She fondled Judith's hair and added huskily, 'You want to please Damian, don't you?'

'Well, yes, I suppose so,' she answered, unable to recall how she got back to her room last night, but disappointed because he wasn't in the bed with her.

'Of course you do. We all seek his approval. Now, get up and we'll begin. Prepare to be amazed,' Anna concluded, holding out a white silk kimono. Judith slipped her arms into it.

Prunella unlocked a door in the wall that Judith had taken to be a cupboard. It opened on to a passageway that connected with other rooms. Now she understood how her nocturnal lover had got in. He hadn't been an incubus after all. It was Damian playing tricks. Her heart leapt and her pussy clenched as she thought about him. She relished the sting of her whipped skin and the ache of the purple bruises marking her buttocks. For all the use the cotton knickers had proved, she might as well have been completely naked. She remembered how he had brought her to orgasm and desire sizzled along her nerve endings. He had rammed his enormous cock up her backside and it had hurt like hell – but she wanted more, with a ravenous hunger that gnawed at her vitals.

Prunella opened another door and Judith was taken into a white room. It contained a bath, a shower stall, and a massage couch covered by a white towel. Phials of rare perfume and jars of unguents provided colour, along with crystal bottles of crushed petals infused with aromatic oils. These stood on glass shelves placed at intervals along the Islamic tiled walls. The air was sweet and fragrant and essentially feminine. A man would have been out of place there.

'Our temple of the mysteries,' Anna said, as if reading Judith's thoughts. 'Here we prepare ourselves for our duties, just like vestal virgins. First of all, I want you to go into the loo and empty yourself. No one will disturb you.'

She pointed to a door and Judith passed through it. It wasn't easy to defecate to order, but she did her best, returning after a short while. The room was moist, steam rising from the surface of the square sunken bath. Judith thought of her Roman sketch, and wondered if Marcus might appear. It seemed that almost anything was possible in the Rectory.

No sweaty gladiator arrived, however, but Anna was there, looking like a surgeon in a loose white, knee-length cotton smock, white shoes, a white cap hiding her hair. Prunella had also changed into a uniform that could have belonged to a nurse or a masseuse.

She removed Judith's kimono and helped her across to the bath. Judith wanted to shake her off and assert her independence. The maid was treating her like an elderly person or a dimwit, her attitude annoyingly patronising. But when Judith stepped into the tub, any reservations vanished. She lowered herself until she was completely immersed. The water was heavenly, warm and frothing and bubbly, her nipples poking above the foam, shining and wet and pert. Prunella rolled back her sleeves, took up a big yellow sponge and started to lather Judith's back. It was unusual but pleasant to have someone else wash her. She'd not experienced this since childhood, and then her mother had always been in a rush, distracted by some business concerning Robert, whose needs always took precedence over his sister's.

Not so in this luxurious bathroom, which might

well have catered for the wants of a sultan's pampered harem. Anna stood near the rim, issuing instructions, and presently Kelly joined her. She was also attired in white. Judith began to feel that she was in a health spa and beauty clinic. When she emerged from the water, she was wrapped in a huge fluffy towel and Prunella shampooed her, using top-of-the-range products, including a conditioner followed by mousse. This thickened her fine hair and made it glossy, encouraging its natural wave. So far, so good. Nothing awful had been done to her; quite the reverse, in fact. She was willing to place herself in their hands.

'Hop up on the couch,' Kelly said encouragingly.

'What now?' Judith asked.

'Pru's going to trim your pussy,' Anna informed her.

This brought Judith up with a start. 'Shave me? But I don't want that. I've never . . . not ever got rid of my bush.'

'Then maybe it's time you did,' Anna said blandly. 'You'll love it once it's done. We won't use a razor, just a depilatory cream, and we won't take it all. We'll leave a pretty little fluffy stripe down the centre. All we're going to do is tidy it up a bit.'

'OK,' Judith conceded reluctantly, and sank down on the couch.

It was rather high, and Prunella lifted back the towel, exposing Judith's sex, then she slithered Judith's torso down until her legs hung over the edge. The maid perched on a stool placed at the end of the bench between Judith's legs. Judith could feel herself blushing with embarrassment at having her cunt so shamelessly exposed to Anna and Prunella. Kelly was somewhere behind Judith's head, but even so, she would be looking at Judith's breasts and down the naked length of her body.

'Wide apart, please, Miss Shaw,' Prunella said with a bright smile. 'That's right. I'm going to spread the cream on the insides of your thighs, though you seem to be hairless there, but we'll trap any stray fronds. I'll smooth it each side of your cleft and on the very edges of your labial lips, leave it for a moment, then scrape it off. You'll be as clean as a new pin.'

'Fresh as a daisy,' chortled Kelly.

'Smooth as a baby's bottom. Just like me,' added Anna, and slowly unbuttoned the front of her smock. The sides fell open and she was naked beneath, except for a pair of white hold-up stockings and her court shoes.

Judith looked at Anna's suntanned pubis, centred by the dark cleft that disappeared into her fork. Her pussy was hairless and bejewelled, the diamond adorning her clitoris glittering invitingly. It was extremely attractive, and Judith relaxed, submitting to Prunella's administrations.

The maid smiled again, and said, 'I use this lotion on madam all the time. It's marvellous stuff, and perfect for sensitive areas.'

The cool, oily cream, the feel of rubber-gloved fingers sliding over her curly pubic hair, the sound of Anna's soft, encouraging voice, all combined to lull Judith into a delicious haze. She felt as if every muscle in her body was melting. As Prunella worked in the cream, the skin around Judith's genitals warmed, sending desire shooting into her clit. She had never felt more exposed or more brazen, and lolled there with her legs as wide as she could spread them, wanting Prunella, Anna and Kelly to look at her treasures. Her vaginal walls pulsed. She was growing wet, and was certain that Prunella would notice her own juices mingling with the depilatory cream.

Her clitoris was stirring, greedy for Prunella's fingers on it, stroking, rubbing, bringing it release. Judith squirmed a little, trying to angle herself towards that ultimate caress, but Prunella seemed unaware, going about her task in a businesslike fashion, stretching the folds slightly in her hunt for stray hairs. Then she sat back.

'All done,' she said. 'Would madam care to inspect?'

Anna leaned over and examined Judith's pubic mound closely. She put out a finger and ran it over the smooth, flushed skin. 'That's fine.'

With firm, sure strokes, Prunella rubbed another scented oil into Judith's mons, then brought over a mirror so that she could see. Propped up on her elbows, she stared at the smooth sweep of the plump hillock that rose so high and fell away so steeply to the concealed mystery below. Not since she reached puberty had she seen it like this – bald and smooth and pink. Yet it wasn't quite the same. Now there was a racy line of fur pointing like an arrow to her clit.

Next Prunella had her move up the padded bench and started to massage her. She was skilled at her job, using the edges of her hands to hammer and rap lightly, then settling down to a more steady rhythm, pinching Judith's muscles, working firmly on her calves, her feet and each toe. Up again, and more oil was applied to her belly, her breasts, her neck and arms. Judith was trembling, unbearably aroused by those professional sweeps of her entire body, the lingering attention to her nipples and breasts, and her receptive thighs. She closed her eyes, longing for Prunella to home in on her clitoris, her sex tingling with the excitement engendered by the removal of its hair, and the sensations now caused by Prunella's glove-free, experienced hands.

Then she felt herself being caressed by others. She looked up into Kelly's face, and saw Anna at the bottom of the couch. 'It's all right,' Anna said comfortingly. 'Don't be afraid. We're going to show you delights that'll blow you apart.'

Her fingers slipped between Judith's thighs and entered her velvety wet channel. Judith gasped at the sensation of those long, agile digits pressing in and out of her, while a thumb flicked over her eager bud. Kelly gently tantalised Judith's nipples until she was almost screaming for completion, strung out on a rack of passionate need. Prunella knelt before her mistress, her face buried in that stunningly lovely cunt, her tongue lapping at the jewel-encrusted clitoris. Anna didn't hesitate. She continued a smooth, perfectly operated caressing of Judith's love-bud until she achieved an orgasm so powerful that Kelly looked down at her, somewhat alarmed.

For long minutes after she had come, Judith continued to writhe, while Anna achieved bliss against Prunella's mouth. Kelly lifted her own gown and rubbed herself to climax. As soon as Anna had recovered, she grabbed Prunella by the hair, hauled her away from her pussy and said, 'Fetch the dildo, slave.'

'Yes, mistress,' Prunella answered humbly, got up from her knees and went to a nearby cupboard.

Limp as a wet rag, Judith didn't want to move, in that lazy, post-orgasm state, but she was startled into action when Prunella reappeared with a large flesh-coloured object that resembled an erect penis. It had a pair of balls at its base, and hummed energetically when Prunella switched it on before handing it to Anna.

'The next phase of your education, Judith,' she said, smock lifted, her legs wide and braced on her high shoes. She licked the buzzing end of the dildo, then ran it across her slick-wet crack and circled the tip of her clitoris. 'Oh, you're in for a treat,' she added and held it towards Judith. 'Here, take a close look. It's a perfect model of a dick – Damian's dick, to be exact, so it'll be custom built for you, darling. See the veins running up its shaft and the bulging, circumcised knob? Let's try it for size.'

Before Judith realised her intention, Anna inserted the throbbing thing into her vagina. Judith gave an astonished yelp as pleasure engulfed her. It felt utterly amazing, a huge, vibrating mass that seemed to tantalise every single nerve in her loins. She almost sobbed when Anna withdrew it, working it along her delta, letting it idle over her clitoris, and then taking it to her nether hole and starting to push it in.

'Ow! That hurts. Please don't do it,' Judith begged, struggling against the weird yet exciting invasion of her privacy.

'Do you want me to use restraints?' Anna asked sternly. 'I shall have to if you don't cooperate.'

'No. Don't tie me. But it hurts so much,' Judith moaned.

At a nod from Anna, Kelly and Prunella leapt upon Judith and held her still while Anna shoved a pillow under Judith's hips, raising them high, and then carried on pushing the dildo into her arse. Judith felt as if she was being impaled, then memories of Damian clicked in. This invasive object felt like his cock, but there was one difference – it was in constant movement, the vibrations seeming to stir her to the bowels. No wonder Anna had ordered her to the lavatory before beginning this alien penetration of her dark nether regions.

Her sphincter clenched. Anna persisted. The dildo

conquered, inch by inch. At last it was fully inserted, the pretend balls touching her bottom. Anna switched it off, and Judith lay there, unable to move and as stuffed as a Christmas turkey.

'Take it out,' she implored, tears trickling from the corners of her eyes and running down to soak into the towel beneath her head.

'Not for an hour,' Anna said crisply. 'And then I'll replace it with a larger plug.'

'You can't do this to me.'

'Damian's orders. And if you're a very good girl, he says you can spend the night in his bed. Isn't that worth a smidgen of discomfort?'

It *was* worth it, Judith thought later, when she was ordered to attend Damian in his magnificent, awesome bedchamber. Candles glowed, and logs sparked and smouldered in the wide hearth. There was something sombre, almost ecclesiastical about the hangings, the tapestries, and the priceless Byzantine icons that adorned the panelled walls. The bed was large and draped in purple, and Damian lounged on its coverlet, made of jaguar pelts.

Music sent demonic vibrations through the air. The CD playing on the hi-fi was the *Mephisto Waltz*. A masterly performance, but not Damian.

'It's Jorge Bolet,' he said, his arms linked behind his head, his body covered by a brocade dressing gown with a sable collar, his bare feet crossed at the ankles. 'You like it?'

'It's wonderful, but I enjoyed your interpretation best,' she said, walking to the fireplace and holding out her hands to the blaze. She was chilled to the marrow, though the house was fully heated. Her nerves were playing merry hell with her.

Kelly had helped her select her clothing, suggesting the simple slip dress she had worn before. Despite her friendship with Anna, Kelly seemed no less protective of Judith. 'I'm helping you to understand yourself,' she had said. 'To come out of your shell. I love you to bits, Jude, and want you to be so confident that you'll spit in any bugger's eye that gives you hassle.'

It was all very well when Kelly was with her, Judith thought, but an entirely different story now that she was here alone in Damian's presence. She was edgy and strung out. She'd seen him at dinner, and then he had vanished. Later, when they were drinking coffee in the salon, Fadil had appeared with a note on a silver salver. It was very much to the point: *Judith, come to my room at once.*

And here she was, trembling before her master, even though she told herself repeatedly that this was absolute nonsense. She was a woman of the twenty-first century, not some concubine.

'Then why are you here?' that sensible little imp asked, perched somewhere on her shoulder.

'I don't know,' she answered in her head.

'Liar, liar, pants on fire,' the imp mocked. 'You want him to shag you legless. He's wickedly exciting, isn't he? Much more so than that berk, Peter.'

'What about Adam?' It was as if she was making excuses to herself.

'Him, too,' said the imp conclusively.

'Judith, come to me,' Damian commanded then, and she couldn't help herself. Of their own volition, her feet moved across the Persian carpet towards the bed.

The *Mephisto Waltz*, its satanic overtones concluded, was followed by the lovely, languorous romanticism of another of Liszt's works, the *Sonata in B minor*.

'This music was used in the orchestral score of Kenneth MacMillan's ballet, *Mayerling*,' she said, and stopped by the bed, filling her eyes and heart with the sight of his extraordinarily handsome features. He was everything she had ever dreamed of in a man – talented, cultured, someone with whom she could share her passion for the arts.

'I know. I saw the 1995 revival at the Royal Opera House,' he said, and his seductive voice wound its way round her heartstrings and into her sex.

'MacMillan died backstage on the opening night,' she said, happy when he reached out and took her hand, winding his fingers through hers.

'What a way to go,' he replied, and drew her down beside him.

'A marvellous way to go,' she agreed, sinking into his arms.

'But we're not here to talk of dying,' he said, running his hands over her body. 'We've come together to celebrate life.'

'Oh, yes, Damian, yes!' she breathed, lifting her face for his kiss. And as his tongue entered her mouth, she dropped her hand down and felt his cock through the thin silk of his robe.

'Do you love me, Judith?' he asked, his tongue caressing her earlobe and that erogenous zone where her shoulders joined her spine. At the same time, he teased one of her breasts through the skimpy bodice.

How could she doubt that what she felt for him was love, not in that perilously seductive moment when he was pulling out all the stops?

'Yes, Damian,' she murmured, arching her ribs to push her breasts into his hands. 'Oh, yes. I think I love you.'

'My darling,' he crooned, and slid down her bootlace shoulder straps, baring her breasts and making her glad she hadn't worn a bra. 'I'm taking you to France. I want you to see my château. The countryside is glorious at this time of the year, and the old place has been in my family for generations. I've often thought that if I ever married, I'd want the ceremony to take place within its ancient walls.'

The vision he painted was so perfect that Judith was borne away on pink marshmallow clouds. Her active imagination supplied the scenery – vineyards and rolling hills and forests . . . a grey château, with round towers and sloping roofs, narrow shuttered windows, and ivy hung walls. And herself in a gorgeous wedding gown (of French design, naturally), and Kelly as a bridesmaid, and possibly Peter, too. She supposed she'd have to include Anna as matron of honour. Then there would be Damian, a sartorial delight in morning coat and top hat. And a priest. Was Damian a Roman Catholic? She wasn't, but would embrace the faith along with everything else when she became his wife.

Then she came to, realising that he hadn't even proposed, and seemed unaware that she had gone off into a dream. He was more interested in removing her clothes, and she helped him to do so, eventually lying naked in his arms and accepting the pleasure that he lavished on her. Emboldened, she tweaked his hard, male nipples, making his cock twitch, then caressed it, sucked it, and formed a channel between her breasts so that he could use them as a mock vagina. She thought herself in heaven.

'Poor little slave,' he whispered, rolling her over and fondling her stripes. 'But these look so inviting against your round bottom, reminding me of the satisfaction I had in punishing you.'

'But you won't do it tonight?' she said, half-hoping he'd say yes.

'Tonight, we are conventional lovers,' he replied, with a cynical lift of his black brows. 'Though I may want to see how efficiently your delicious arsehole has been stretched.'

'Enough, I think,' she said, marvelling at her boldness, and at the quick stab of passion his words evoked.

He concentrated on her pleasure, giving her repeated orgasms, plunging into her love channel with his stiff and apparently tireless cock, then, later, using it to test her back passage. Languid with love, Judith let him do as he wished with her. Not only physical passion but emotional highs held her in thrall. She was in love for the very first time. It hurt. It ached. It was breathtaking. She thought briefly of what Kelly had said about this strange insanity, but thrust it from her mind.

As she lay nestled against Damian's shoulder and he ran his fingers down her belly and admired her bare mons for the umpteenth time, he said gently, 'When we reach Paris, there's someone I want you to meet. He's a business associate. His name is Philippe Laveau. He's very rich and very knowledgeable. I shall introduce you to him and I want you to please him.'

Judith was too sleepy to take in the full import of this, but a sudden chill breeze seemed to play over her skin. 'What d'you mean . . . please him?' she asked.

Damian chuckled, and trailed a finger down the furry arrow leading to her sex. 'Just that, sweetheart. By pleasing him, you please me, and you want to do that, don't you?'

'Yes, Damian,' she murmured, lifting her hips from the bed towards that questing digit.

'Good girl,' he said, and passed through the arrow to find her clit.

'What's a nice girl like you doing in a place like this?' asked the suntanned, lean and rugged man that Kelly had been edging towards. He was the most interesting thing that had happened all evening, even though she was at a cocktail party in the magnificent house of financier and art critic Philippe Laveau, situated in the most prestigious residential area of Paris.

'I'm working for Damian Cresswell. He's on a buying trip, amongst other things,' she said, liking the stranger's American drawl. She looked him over and decided that he was even more sexy close up than when she'd spotted him on the other side of the room.

'Anna and Damian, the Heavenly Twins,' he commented with a touch of irony.

'You know them?'

'I sure do. Everyone knows them in the close-knit realms of erotica collecting. I'm Jake Bryce, salvage expert and general dealer in anything old, interesting and valuable. What's your name?'

He was looking at her from under his lashes. His eyes were dark blue, sharp, at odds with his lazy, easy-going demeanour. His hair was brown and straight, reaching the neckband of his collarless grandad shirt. Everyone else was in semi-formal attire. The women oozed Parisian chic, most of them wearing the almost obligatory little black dress. The men were sleek in Italian tailored suits and Gucci shoes, but Jake's slim hips and long thighs were encased in blue jeans. He wore no jacket and the full sleeves of the white shirt gave him a rakish air. To add to this impression, his denims were tucked into the tops of knee-high burgundy leather boots.

His jaw was stubbled – not a fashion statement, Kelly was sure, but a genuine lack of razor application, either because he was too busy or because he didn't give a toss. A swashbuckler and a show-off, she decided, prepared to dislike him, her defences going up with a clang, but so excited that she creamed her panties.

'I'm Kelly Cameron,' she said, and held out her hand.

He shook it, and held it a tad longer than was necessary before releasing it and saying, 'Pleased to meet you. Can I get you a drink? How about a margarita? The best damn cocktail ever invented. The only way to drink tequila, and I've tried 'em all, believe me.'

She didn't doubt this, though she could see he wasn't a drinking man. He looked too fit. She visualised him in Peru or the Amazonian jungle or scouring the Caribbean Sea in his salvage boat, a hard-bitten adventurer. She could even imagine him offering his services as a mercenary in skirmishes between foreign states. She dropped her gaze to his hands, strong hands with broad palms and sinewy backs, and thought, I'll bet he's a crack shot.

'Tequila sunrise is OK,' she said. She'd drunk that with Alden Ray in what now seemed a hundred years ago.

Events had accelerated since Damian's party and Judith's indoctrination: a week working for Adam, packing, switching on the cottage's security alarms and alerting the Neighbourhood Watch, then getting it together to travel by Eurostar. Damian had booked rooms in the fabulous, two-hundred-year-old Hôtel de Crillon, in the Place de la Concorde. He had given them little time for sightseeing or shopping, but had hustled them to the famous flea markets to hunt for bargains. It was all heady stuff. Kelly hadn't visited France since going on a school trip as a teenager, though it had been a far cry from this. She had sent postcards of the Eiffel Tower to Caroline and Sally, who were green with envy, thinking she'd be having a ball. She wasn't exactly – or not until now, at any rate.

The salon of Laveau's establishment was the last word in luxury, sumptuously decorated with chandeliers, original sculptures, gilt mouldings, tapestries and inlaid furniture. Kelly hadn't yet been introduced to her host. He, Damian and Anna were incarcerated in the study, as close as conspirators, leaving Judith, Peter and herself to their own devices.

And that suits me fine, Kelly concluded, her sex stirring as Jake returned with their drinks and they found a quiet spot in the glass-enclosed terrace where they could get to know one another undisturbed. Tingling with more than just the infusion of tequila and orange liqueur in her blood, Kelly sat down on a wrought-iron garden seat and inclined her slightly parted knees towards him. Her black sequinned skirt rode high over fishnet stockings with lacy hold-ups, and her feet looked amazingly slim and elegant in the black, stilt-heeled shoes. Her top was a black velvet halter-neck, displaying her shoulders, the hollows of her throat and her rounded breasts where the hardened nipples raised the material into two stiff points. She had fluffed out her chestnut hair into a mass of ringlets, and fastened gold Creole hoops in her ears.

It was about time that she had a man again. The titillation she'd experienced at the fancy-dress party, the witnessing of S&M sex dramas, the knowledge that she could have Anna, or even Damian, was not enough. Alden had proved boring in the long run, but Jake shared some of the rock star's smouldering attraction, that hint of danger lurking beneath the surface, that element of unpredictability. She liked his eloquent hands, his mouth, the promise of muscle beneath his shirt, the even greater promise of what lay behind the fly of his Levi's. But there was one question she had to ask. It was her policy never to mess with married men.

She came right out with it. 'Is your wife with you?'

He gave a quirky smile. 'I don't have one. "He travels fastest who travels alone." What about you?'

'No, I don't have a wife,' she teased, surprised at how pleased she was that he was single.

One of his eyebrows shot up, his eyes twinkling with amusement. 'A husband, then?'

'No husband either.'

'A partner? A significant other?'

'No.'

'Great. You come from England?' he asked, and one finger stroked her bare shoulder in a way that made her quiver.

'That's right. The West Country. And you're from the States?'

'The Deep South. New Orleans to be precise. My mother is a genuine Cajun lady. My real name is Jacques, but Jake is easier all round.'

'I've always wanted to go there.'

'I'll take you. I've a house in the French Quarter. It's old, mysterious, steeped in history. We could visit the swamps where the trees are hung with ghostly Spanish moss and alligators live out their lives as a protected species. The days are humid and the nights are hot. It isn't a place for the faint-hearted, but I guess you're not, Kelly Cameron.'

It was as if he was issuing a challenge, and she wanted to take it up, but not quite yet. He shouldn't

154

have it all his own way. 'I don't know about that,' she said. 'I've just started a new job. I do computer work for Adam Renald. He runs the Falcon Bookshop in Salisbury. Do you know him?'

'I have come across him with Damian. Thick as thieves those two, and Anna as well. But I don't want to talk about them, I want know about you, Kelly. I'm serious about you coming to Louisiana with me,' he said, moving along the bench until his thigh was brushing hers. He slid an arm behind her shoulders and she was surprised by how right it felt.

'You're a fast worker,' she chided with a laugh. 'What a chat-up line!'

'Don't try to tell me you're not used to being chatted up,' he mocked gently, and the light in his blue eyes ignited an answering fire inside her. 'You're wrong about me. I'm serious. Seems to me we'd make a great team.'

'What a load of crap! How can you tell? We've only known each other five minutes. I've been around, I've got your number,' she retorted, determined not to be diverted by sentimentality or emotion, but to get down to what they both wanted: a pure, unadulterated fuck.

Without giving him the opportunity to answer, she sat astride his lap, her skirts high, her pubis pressed to the erection straining his jeans. He watched her with those keen eyes, put a hand behind her head and drew her mouth towards his. His kiss shook her to the core. It was a deep, satisfying kiss. His tongue probed between her lips and lazily explored her teeth, gums and palate. It coiled with hers, tangled and tickled and stimulated until she was moaning her pleasure into his mouth.

He unclipped the halter that fastened at the back of

her neck and, without its support, the top slid down below her breasts. He held back a little to admire them, his full lips smiling, before he leaned forward and sucked first one, then the other, his wet finger flickering over the abandoned nipple, doubling the sensation. Kelly gasped and bore down against his prick. She wanted to see it, to feel it, to free it from its confinement. She unbuckled his belt, seized the tag of his zipper and eased it down. His cock sprang out, its girth and length all she could have hoped for, and there was something else, too. He was pierced. A gold ring ran through the slit at the tip and came out again just where his foreskin rolled back.

A pang of fierce lust darted through Kelly. 'Wow!' she exclaimed. 'This'll be a first.'

'Never been fucked by a guy with a Prince Albert before? You'll love it, honey. It's great. Increases sensation for both,' he promised, and pushed aside the thin gusset of her knickers, combing a finger through her bush and circling her clit with soft, irresistible movements.

'Why is it called a Prince Albert?' she asked, moving the ring slowly. It was slippery with pre-come.

'The story goes that your Queen Victoria's consort wore one to hold back the skin of his uncut prick, making it easier to clean,' he said, grimacing with pleasure at the sensation. 'And guys used it as a way of keeping their cocks under control, so as not to stick out when wearing tight, fashionable pants. They slipped a cord through the ring and anchored it along their inseams. Hell, just think of the restraint!'

She closed her hand round his shaft. He slid lower so that his glans filled her fist and the ring rotated against her palm. He groaned, and she was afraid she wasn't doing it right. She'd had men with piercings, of course – ears, eyebrows, lips, nipples – but never through their cocks. It had taken an American to teach her that juicy item of English history.

'Is this how you like it?' she murmured.

'Yes, yes,' he hissed urgently. 'That's it, sugar. But not too much or this will be over before we've begun. Hey, wait a second while I get this on.'

'Let me do it,' she whispered, and took the prophylactic from him, snapped open the packet and carefully rolled the clear plastic over his glans and down his shaft.

She raised herself, straddling him, guiding the domed head to her entrance. He lifted his hips and pushed. His cock went halfway in. Her panties were well out of the way to one side and she was copiously wet. Jake began rolling his thumb over her clit and she was close to the edge. Slowly, she impaled herself on his cock, squatting and letting it slide in deeper, until she could feel the end nudging her cervix, deep inside. She rode him, shifting up and down, her pleasure mounting at the feel of that large organ filling her, and the acute delight as he frigged her bud. She lifted her hands and cupped her bare breasts, her fingers pulling at the nipples, making them crimp and ache.

This guy was good! If being a tough loner turned a man into such a skilled lover, then she'd recommend it – strongly.

His face wore an absorbed expression, and she liked the planes and hollows, shadows and highlights of his features. Not exactly handsome, he was wildly desirable, nonetheless, particularly when he was rousing her clit in that adroit manner, while pumping up into her in heavy, steady strokes. She was almost there, the force gathering in her loins, her nubbin pulsing. A fraction more and she strained to hang on to the comet tail of orgasm as it streamed past her.

'Come on, *cher*. Come for me. I want to feel you do it,' he muttered huskily in that southern accent which dripped with honey. That was all it took. She was there, sobbing, shaken by one of the best orgasms of all time. And he was still cupping her mound, still whispering fiery words, saying, 'Ride me! Jeez, you feel tight as a velvet glove inside. Go on. Milk me dry.'

She felt his cock jerk as her vaginal muscles convulsed round it, and that added heat and force as he ejaculated into the condom. He sighed and pulled her close, pressing his face between her breasts. The world righted itself, and Kelly was once again aware that there was a party going on just behind the patio doors. Anyone could come out there at any moment. She swung a leg over his lap and got to her feet. Her panties had worked up into her bottom crease, and she wriggled to get them into a more comfortable position, but her pussy was very wet, and the crotch was soon soaked. She managed to adjust her hold-ups, then looked down at Jake.

He still lay sprawled on the bench, flaccid cock outside the opening of his jeans. The ring glistened with juice. He looked for all the world like a sated lion who had just gorged himself on the best part of an antelope. He was smiling at her, his eyes heavy-lidded. 'That sure was something else,' he said, taking off the rubber and dropping it into the pot of a splendid, lush and tropical plant that stood handy.

'I'm going back,' she announced with a cool she was far from feeling. To her dismay, she found that she wanted to see him again.

'Right,' he said, zipped up and moved to stand by

her, all in one easy movement. 'I'll come with you. Can't wait to see Damian and find out what goddamn plot he's hatching.'

Chapter 8

'MY ASSISTANT, MISS JUDITH Shaw,' Damian said, leading her towards the dapper, rotund man standing by the fireplace in the study. Anna was seated in a wing-back chair nearby, her black chiffon gown rescued from total immodesty by the judicial placing of jet-beaded embroidery.

'Ah, the girl you've been speaking of,' Philippe Laveau replied, raising a bushy eyebrow at Anna, who smiled in return. He took Judith's hand in his, lifting it to his slack, wet lips.

He was around fifty, with thinning dark hair, and not much taller than her. He couldn't restrain the lecherous leer that slid over florid features that had once been handsome but had now gone to seed. His command of the English language was faultless, as was his pale grey silk and wool suit, cut on generous, baggy lines, not so much for the sake of fashion as to facilitate his generous proportions. In other words, Philippe was fat.

Damian's lips curved sardonically, his eyes guarded as he considered the interplay between the Frenchman and Judith. He almost experienced a qualm of conscience. She was so gullible. It seemed hardly cred-

160

ible in this age of feisty, ball-breaking females that fate should have cast such a one in his path. Her sincerity touched him and he didn't like this, considering it a weakness on his part. He shut his mind to guilt. *Carpe diem*, he thought: Seize the day. He had come here to get something, and he didn't intend to leave France without it.

The photograph! He'd seen it once and once only, but the urge to possess it had given him no rest, and he'd been chasing it ever since. He remembered how Philippe had gloated when he showed it to him. So rare a thing, and so valuable. The only one of its kind in existence, produced by Paul Antoine, the acknowledged master of this type of work, highly skilled, artistic and salacious. Many of his photographs and their glass plates had been seized by the French police, deemed to be obscene and destroyed. This added to the value of any that had escaped this act of vandalism.

The picture was called *Mademoiselle Ninette* and, as far as Damian recalled, it epitomised that era of double standards, when women of the lower orders were poor, and gentlemen of the upper echelons only too willing to pay for their favours. Damian had moved mountains in order to add this gem to his collection. Philippe drove a hard bargain. He wasn't over-eager to sell and didn't need the money. Damian had been seeking an inducement that would tip the balance. Judith.

Along with his greed to possess unique items, so Philippe lusted after lovely young women. Of course, he could have as many as he wanted, were it not for a quirk. It was essential for his satisfaction that they were artless, even unworldly, and this was a rarity. He got his jollies by besmirching innocence and bending his victims to his will. Damian didn't know him all that well, but considered him to be conceited and stupid, no match for his own razor-sharp wit.

He had spent time that evening whetting Philippe's appetite, painting Judith as an unsophisticated lass from the heart of rural England. It seemed he had succeeded in arousing the man's lust, for he was staring at her with a drooling expression, hardly able to keep his stubby fingers off her. Damian's cynical smile deepened. *Mademoiselle Ninette* was as good as his.

'Judith would very much like to see your photographs,' he said, judging Philippe's state of arousal carefully.

'Would you, my dear?' Philippe asked, cupping her elbow and inviting her to sit on the cane and uphol-stered bergère settee, then settling himself beside her, pressing close although there was plenty of space.

'I'm interested in anything antique,' she said, shooting Damian a pleading glance. He ignored it. The meeting was going better than he could have hoped. Philippe was impressed, his eagerness betrayed by the way his erection was lifting the front of his trousers under the round pumpkin of his belly.

'Ah, yes ... history and art and objects produced years ago, when genuine craftsmen still existed,' he cooed, and placed a podgy hand on her knee. 'You like looking at erotic prints? It excites you? Makes you want to be naughty, eh?'

Anna exchanged a glance with Damian. He knew she was thinking the same as him: Philippe was putty in their hands.

Judith was struggling, Damian could tell. This was totally outside her experience, but she would obey him, he was sure. He hadn't told her the details, only

162

that he wanted her to do whatever Philippe required. He knew she was struggling against her revulsion for the Frenchman with his oily manner and unattractive personality, to say nothing of his gross figure. The idea of her forcing herself to obey sent prickles of desire straight down Damian's spine to his penis. He could feel it hardening beneath his form-fitting black trousers. It surged with the power he enjoyed above all, his mastery over his new slave, his successful manipulation of Philippe. This was meat and drink to him.

'I've told Judith about *Mademoiselle Ninette*,' he said, blandly. 'Would you permit her to look at it?'

Philippe's eyes shone like small brown pebbles, and he ventured a hand into Judith's bodice, squeezing her breast as he answered, 'That can be arranged. But first, I want to see her pussy. Just a glimpse, that's all for now.'

Damian nodded at Judith and saw her hands trembling as she slid her skirt up over her thighs with a genuine shyness that was stimulating. He'd commanded that she wear nothing under the dress, apart from stockings, and as the hem rose higher, the tops of her thighs showed, and then her fork, with its fascinating, central stripe of neatly clipped hair.

Philippe's gasp was audible. He leaned over, staring at that enticing view. 'I can smell it,' he enthused, his jowls quivering like a barnyard rooster's, little beads of sweat breaking out on his brow. 'I want to touch it.'

'Not yet,' Damian said crisply. 'The photograph first.'

Philippe dragged his eyes away from Judith's crotch. 'As you wish, *monsieur*,' he said, and got to his feet. He clapped his hands and two bulky, shaven-headed bodyguards appeared. They wore evening suits, and could have been butlers or wine waiters, had it not been for the revolvers bulking out their jackets. Damian knew that Philippe relied on his personal army; too rich, influential and disliked to feel safe unless surrounded by heavies.

The guards walked on either side of Philippe as he conducted his guests down a long corridor to a flight of steps that led to the basement. This was a new venue for Damian. He'd visited Philippe on several occasions but had never been taken to his strong room, where they eventually arrived.

He's taking a chance, even when heavily protected, Damian thought, as Philippe approached one of the solid iron safes cemented into the wall. Is he so cunt-struck that he's blind to anything else? All right, so it would be dangerous, but I could break in here now I know the way. The massive wall box Philippe selected was another matter. One would have to know the code, or blow it up – not impossible if one employed a professional safe-cracker. But why should I want to do that, apart from for the sheer hell of it? he asked himself. If Philippe lets me have the photo, then I'll go away quietly and leave him in peace.

The bodyguards were alert, balancing on sturdy legs, their faces those of prize-fighters, with broken noses and cauliflower ears. Anna was looking them over, and Damian guessed she'd like to take up the gauntlet and see if it was possible to seduce them from their duty. This might prove useful one day. Philippe was blissfully ignorant of any foul intent. His hands were fluttering over the mechanism that protected his safe. Only himself and his banker were cognisant with the password and computerised numeric sequence.

A sharp click signified success, and he swung open the heavy door. A light came on inside, illumining

164

shelves filled with caskets of jewels, cash boxes, gold ingots, documents and original sketches by famous, long dead artists. There were other things, too: a whole medley of mounted photographs carefully stashed in protective coverings. He selected one, and beckoned Judith to him.

She hesitated and Damian prodded her. She joined the portly Frenchman and he handed her the daguerreotype. She stared down at it. Damian watched her face. She was flustered and, he hazarded a guess, creaming her snatch. The photograph would have excited her. He moved across to where she stood, and leaned over her shoulder.

The combination of circumstances – Judith's body, her musky scent, the sight of *Mademoiselle Ninette*, who was even more enchanting than he recalled – made his cock twitch and harden. He exercised superb control, feasting on the photograph of the saucy, ebony-haired model seated brazenly on the back of a *chaise-longue*, legs wide and bent at the knee, her feet braced in black button boots, her hands holding open her fluff-fringed labial wings and displaying a larger than average clitoris. She smiled down at her male lover who lay below her, gazing up at the spectacle, his trousers wrinkled round his hips, his hand clasping his erect penis. Another girl, stripped of everything save her black stockings, garters and Louis heeled shoes, was leaning over from behind and fingering Ninette's nipples.

It was all that Damian remembered, and much, much more.

'Do you accept my offer, Laveau?' he asked, unable to keep the urgency from his voice.

'What was it? Twenty thousand pounds?' the Frenchman demurred.

'Yes, dammit. That's the sum we discussed.'

Philippe pulled a dubious face and smoothed the line of moustache that lay like a black slug beneath his prominent nose. 'I'm not sure. It's in perfect condition. No fading, no blotches. It could have been taken yesterday. I'd get far more for it in America.'

'But you wouldn't get the chance to sample a perfect gem from my own private collection,' Damian said, and put his arm round Judith and walked her forward until she was within an inch of Philippe, her breasts brushing against his chest. 'She's dear to me, but I'm willing to share her with you, if you accept my offer. Do we have a bargain?'

He ran a hand down Judith's back as he spoke, and let his fingers penetrate the crack between her buttocks, barely covered by the flimsy material of her dress. He felt her thrust her bottom up, seeking more caresses. He bent and placed his lips on the side of her neck, and she arched, throwing back her head and sighing. He nibbled, using those vampire kisses that he knew aroused her to screaming pitch. She made no objection when Philippe hitched up her skirt and grabbed her pussy, squeezing and feeling it. He grunted as he did so, and ground his penis against her thigh.

'I must admit to being more than a little tempted,' he said. 'For how long can I have her?'

'I'm travelling to my château and shall be staying there for a few days. Why don't you come with me and enjoy her?' Damian suggested, though it stuck in his craw to pander to the objectionable little man.

'She'll be mine for the duration of my visit?'

'Yes,' Damian agreed.

'Your château? Is it well equipped?' Philippe asked slyly, his hand still ferreting around between Judith's legs.

'Naturally. Its torture chamber and playthings are second to none. I'll put it at your disposal.'

'And I can bring my own people with me, and do anything I want with the girl?'

'It will be my pleasure,' Damian said, and gave an ironic bow.

He was surprised and satisfied to notice that Judith had apparently cottoned on to his scheme. She was responding to Philippe without being told, grabbing his stubby cock and rubbing it through his trousers.

Anna winked at Damian and turned to leave. 'I'll let you get on with your transaction,' she said. 'I'm going back to the party. See you later.'

Damian gave her a cursory nod and concentrated on Philippe. 'Well? Shall I write out a cheque?' he asked.

'I'd appreciate a sample first,' Philippe prevaricated. 'Is she an expert at fellatio?'

Damian nodded and snapped his fingers at Judith. 'Do as he wants,' he said.

Distrustful, and determined to keep an eye on his property, Damian leaned back against the wall, arms folded over his chest, feet crossed at the ankles. Philippe flopped down in a massive throne-like chair, one of several pieces of antique furniture in the strong room. He opened his trousers and eased his ample buttocks forward a little, lifting his hips to give greater access to his testicles and cock.

Judith dropped down between his spread knees. His penis curved upwards from beneath his paunch, the foreskin pulled back. It wasn't a long prick, but its girth was ample, and it rose jauntily from a nest of scrubby black hair. Damian glanced at it disparagingly. It made him proud of his own impressive endowment. Somehow the sight of Judith in that submissive pose drove him wild with passion. She delicately scratched over Philippe's balls, weighed and played with them until his member elongated considerably.

'Oh, that's marvellous,' he groaned, and buried his hands in her hair, drawing her down to his groin. 'Ah, the things we'll do at the château, the games we'll play. There's so much I want you to try. But for now, take me into your lovely mouth.'

He gave a jerk and she was face down in his lap, his pelvis rocking as he thrust his cock between her lips and she slurped on it in ever increasing movements, until he suddenly erupted, spewing semen. It spurted, dribbling down her chin and cheeks and hanging like pearls in her hair. She squatted on her heels, wiping his emission away with the back of her hand. Damian was disturbed to see her savage expression and the fierce light in her eyes as she glared at Philippe.

It occurred to him that he might be pushing her too far. Then he dismissed this with a shrug. The girl was infatuated with him, wasn't she? She'd carry out his orders, or earn his severe disapproval and be punished.

'Jake! Darling! Where did you spring from?' Anna cried, throwing herself into his arms.

'Here and there and everywhere. You know how it is, honey,' he answered, considering her with his sharp blue eyes.

'I do indeed,' she pouted, and playfully tweaked his nipples through his shirt. 'You're a horrid, wanton, will-o'-the-wisp kind of creature. Now you see me, now you don't. Watch this one, Kelly, and don't believe a word he says.'

'As if,' Kelly snapped, a trifle too quick in springing to her own defence.

'Unfair,' Jake grumbled with a grin, clasping Anna round the arse and pulling her against him, hard.

It was such a familiar caress that her memory went into overdrive. She and Jake had crossed swords before, two well-matched contenders in the cut and thrust of wheeling and dealing, to say nothing of the rutting heat of the bed.

'True, nonetheless,' she said, lightly kissing his lips and then adding, 'What are you doing in Paris?'

'The same as you, sugar. A bit of business. Getting laid.'

'Well, you haven't laid me,' she reminded him, with a reproachful look.

'Not yet. Easy, babe. There's plenty of time.'

'Not so much. I'm off to the Loire Valley tomorrow. Why don't you come? We're already quite a party ... Kelly, who I see you've already met and probably balled ... Judith, who you haven't ... Then there's Damian and me and a guy named Peter, though I sometimes call him Fifi ... Philippe Laveau, to say nothing of servants and subs.'

'Sounds a gas.'

'You'll come?'

'I'll think about it.'

'Don't leave it too long or we'll be gone, heading for the south and sunshine.'

'What is it with Laveau, anyway? I didn't think you'd be cosying up with that freak,' Jake said, a quizzical frown drawing his elfish brows together.

'You know how it is,' Anna drawled. 'One sometimes has to suffer buffoons like him in order to clinch a deal.'

'And what are you after this time?'

169

'Not me,' she answered airily, leaning into him, the jet beading hardly concealing the hard points of her nipples as they contacted his shirt front. 'Damian has his eye on a photograph Philippe owns. He's offering him a small fortune for it, and giving him the use of his newest slave.'

'Ah, still the master, eh?' Jake said, and his blue eyes turned steely.

'Always the master,' she conceded softly, winding her arms round his neck. 'But I can be the mistress, as you very well know. No one owns me unless I want him to.'

'And which photograph is Damian after? Could it be the one they call *Mademoiselle Ninette*?' Jake asked, his fingers toying with the blonde fronds of hair at the nape of her neck.

She pulled away, staring up at him, her violet eyes flashing. 'How do you know about it?'

'It's no secret. Philippe has been boasting about owning it for years, and rumours are flying around that your cousin has put in a bid.'

Jake shrugged and placed an arm round Kelly's slim waist. Anna was even more certain that they'd already fucked. She didn't really care. Jake had only ever been a passing fancy, but even so she liked to be the most desirable woman in the vicinity. It wasn't surprising that he'd turned up at Philippe's party. Many of the guests were international dealers and Jake was well known for cocking a snook at authority and supplying buyers with goods that were, if not exactly red-hot, then warm enough to scorch the fingers of those unlucky enough to be caught; he never was, well versed in greasing palms and bending rules.

She smiled to herself. He'd be an entertaining addition to the house party at the château. Though she had several options for sexual gratification, Jake was something special. She wished she'd watched him screwing Kelly. Where had they done it? In the conservatory? Yes, that was about his mark. He got off on novelty settings. Fun and games, she thought, a frisson of excitement tingling round her pussy. We'll make up a threesome, Kelly and Jake and me.

Peter was getting used to left-hand driving. When they'd arrived in France he'd been totally confused, slavishly following Fadil, who was in charge of the Mercedes, while Peter brought up the rear in the Jaguar. They'd occupied the cars during the journey beneath the English Channel. Prunella had been with them, keeping an eye on the luggage, while Damian and his party enjoyed the luxury of being foot passengers in the plush interior that was reminiscent of the Pullman cars of The Orient Express.

Now they had left Paris, heading for the Loire Valley, and Peter was more confident once he no longer had to negotiate the hectic boulevards and narrow side streets of the capital, with its manic drivers who must have invented road rage. He had taken one look at the city and, despite its impressive monuments, disliked it intensely. Many people found it romantic. He didn't, objecting to its inhabitants who thought themselves superior, its mercenary bent and the smell of drains from which it was impossible to escape.

Fadil had gone through the map with him before they set out, and they were travelling to Blois, the nearest town to Damian's ancestral pile, the Château Scorville. It was a relief to leave the city behind and head out towards the country. Peter was acutely aware of Kelly in the passenger seat, with Judith in the rear.

Fadil was chauffeuring Damian, Anna and Prunella. That newcomer, the oddball American called Jake, was in his own vehicle, a sturdy Shogun FWD. Philippe and his entourage made up the rest of the cortège. This consisted of three cars containing the man himself, his clothes and a gaggle of servants. He never travelled light.

Peter settled down for the two-hour journey, his hands caressing the wheel of a far superior car than he'd ever dreamed he'd be driving. When Anna had invited him to France, his first thought had been: I can't. There's the workshop. There's mother. What am I going to tell her? But Anna was a most persuasive woman, and he was her slave, after all. He'd put his reliable carpenter in charge and told mother very firmly that he needed a holiday.

'But we're off to the Lake District in a few weeks,' she'd complained, standing in the kitchen in that domineering way that reminded him of Anna, arms akimbo, knuckles plonked on her ample hips. 'I thought we might take that nice Judith with us, too.'

'We've been there every year for as long as I can remember,' he'd said, daring to argue. 'I'm sick of it. I want to go somewhere else. I've been invited to stay with friends.'

'Where?' His mother had narrowed her eyes and glared at him.

'France,' he'd said, and it was only the thought of his Fifi outfit that kept him going.

'*France?*' she had bellowed, as if he was proposing a visit to Sodom and Gomorrah.

'Yes. France. There's nothing you can say that'll stop me. I'm going,' he had shouted, astonishing her so much that her mouth had shut like a rat-trap.

It had been a small but significant triumph. He was

eternally grateful to Anna and Kelly for making him their slave instead of his mother's and, in so doing, granting him the boon of independence. The driving seat was warm under his bottom and he was aware of his silky knickers rubbing against his balls and cock. He wore chinos over them, hiding the garter-belt and stockings, while his shirt concealed a lace-edged chemise. Every time he moved an arm, the fabric slithered over his wine-red nipples, making them tighten like little buttons. He quivered with anticipation of the treats to come when they reached the château. Anna had waxed lyrical about the dungeons. The skin of his buttocks became hotter, remembering the trauma of being whipped.

His cock was semi-erect, its customary condition these days, and he wanted to show it to Kelly. He was like a man with a dual personality. One side of him still loved Judith and dreamed of wedding bells, a thatched cottage, of coming home to her at night, and perhaps fathering a couple of kids. Mother would be over the moon to be a grandma. Then there was the other side, the one that had recently shot into prominence – the closet transvestite who had come out, the submissive who wanted to grovel at Mistress Anna's feet and lick her boots, her fanny, and anything else she desired, his pleasure to serve her and be flogged in return.

'Keep your eyes on the road,' Kelly commanded, and her hand came to rest on his knee, then slid higher, touching the bulge behind his flies. She glanced at Judith in the driving mirror, smiling and adding, 'Did you ever guess he was such a little tinker? Just goes to show.'

Judith leaned forward, unclicking her seat belt. 'I know. I'd never have thought you were into cross-dressing, Peter. Why didn't you tell me? I find it a turn on.'

'I didn't like to,' he mumbled.

'There's been a lot of weird happenings since we met the Cresswells. How are you getting along with Philippe?' Kelly asked her. 'If he comes on too strong, then call in the cavalry, kiddo. I'll knee him in the bollocks.'

Peter's ears pricked up. He didn't mind Judith screwing other men, not any more and not at that moment, though he might feel different later, when this fantasy was over. Her face in the mirror looked troubled, and she sank back into the seat and fastened up.

'It's OK. He's only wanted me to give him head once, and if it pleases Damian and helps him to obtain his heart's desire, then I can put up with it,' she said quietly, and Peter was struck by the sudden revelation that he didn't know her any more – had never really known her.

This thought was still with him when, after a short break in Blois, they reached the village of Mer in the slumberous green midlands of France, and knew that their journey was almost over. Mer had once belonged to the feudal lords of the Château Scorville.

Am I lonely? Judith thought. Well, not exactly. There are far too many of us for that, eating and gambling and fornicating and bumping into one another and the servants in the narrow passageways of the château. But sometimes one could feel really alone in a crowd of jolly companions, if all one longed for was the company of a special person.

In what seemed to her to be an act of betrayal, although she knew the reason behind it, Damian had given her to Philippe when they arrived. It had happened in the Great Hall that resembled a hunting museum, hung with trophies: deer heads and boars' heads and foxes and wolves. It was dedicated to war, too: crossed pikes and shields and ragged banners commemorating battles long ago. There was even a dummy dressed as a knight in armour seated on a model horse, also fully caparisoned.

And in this setting, with its giant stone fireplaces, tapestries, paintings and splendidly timbered ceiling, she had witnessed Philippe and Damian concluding their transaction. Damian had handed over a cheque, and she had heard Philippe say, 'She's mine, then?'

'For a week,' Damian had answered, and without glancing in her direction had turned on his heel, whistled to the deer-hounds who had loped over hopefully, lifting their great grey muzzles for his caresses, and left the Great Hall with the dogs in his wake.

Judith had been dispatched to the Frenchman's chamber and chained to the bedpost, awaiting his pleasure. She was later released and allowed to change for dinner in her own room, a lovely place with windows overlooking the formal garden, with its parterres, fountains and stone statuary of naked mythological deities.

Philippe had acted in a proprietorial manner during dinner, and afterwards in the gaming room, goosing her whenever he fancied, fingering her breasts and cunt. That night she was again chained to his bed, but it had passed without him being there, the roulette wheel taking precedence over sex. She had hardly slept a wink, the uncertainty worse than if he'd been constantly fucking her. Next morning she had been freed, and mingled with the others, driving into Blois, having lunch in a quaint bistro, visiting a vineyard and sampling the wine, watching Damian from afar. She had purchased a picture postcard and sent it to Adam, missing that donnish man who had initiated her into the byways of sex, where pleasure could be mingled with pain.

The second night had been spent in bondage, and Philippe had insisted that she watch while he masturbated. Next day he decreed that she might take the air on the top of the tower reached from outside his room by a spiral staircase.

He had ordered her to strip and a member of his staff, a tall, gaunt, androgynous valet called Jay, had wound leather straps around her breasts and body while Philippe gloated on her nudity and ran his fleshy tongue over his full lips. Then he had taken up a pair of gold nipple clamps and fastened them to her tits, pulling on the chain that linked them. The teeth had pinched, her nipples swelling between them, hurting and aching and arousing desire in her.

She still wore these strange devices, as well as the leather thongs, chilled as she stood in the wind that whipped round the crenellated tower. Breathing deeply, she stood under the cross-braced timbers of the conical roof and gazed down at Damian's domain. Fertile meadows and lush fields stretched as far as the eye could see. Once a tributary of the River Loire must have washed the rocks below, but it had withdrawn ages ago, lost in marshlands where the reeds grew thick and the silence was broken at intervals by bird calls and crickets and frogs. Beyond this Judith could see nothing but trees, and a church spire in the far distance beyond the forest.

She nearly shot over the edge of the parapet when someone grabbed her from behind. Familiar hands, familiar smell, cigar smoke and aftershave and a hint of leather.

' "Magic château", as Alfred de Vigny called Chambord in *Cinq-Mar*. That's how I feel about this place,' said Damian, his breath tickling her ear. 'You like it, too?'

'If it wasn't for Philippe, yes, I'd like it fine,' she replied, her heart pounding as he slid a hand in front of her to hold her waist while the other glided to her breast.

He paused, fingering the nipple clamps, and pleasure swamped her body, enflamed but not satisfied by Philippe's antics. 'He did this?' Damian asked.

'He did, with the help of that odd creature, Jay. Is it a man or a woman?'

'I wonder if it knows itself? Philippe boasts that Jay is a hermaphrodite. But not long now, darling,' he promised, and she could feel his bare penis pressing into the small of her back, and then he bent his knees and it was nudging between her buttocks where nothing but a thong protected her.

'Thank God for that!' she exclaimed, rejoicing as he explored the leather binding. The touch of his cool fingers on the heated folds of her labia was wonderful. She leaned forward, thrusting her bottom against his stalk as he shoved two fingers inside her, moving them in and out in a delicious rhythm and then rubbing the sliver of flesh crowning her slit.

He pushed the thong aside and his prick nosed into her wet channel. He paused with just the tip inside, then, still rubbing her clit, plunged into the hilt. The extreme pleasure of it, combined with the friction on her bud and her emotional entanglement with him, toppled her over into a massive orgasm that seemed to go on and on and on . . .

He lifted her, had her bend over for him, and she leaned against the stone parapet, groaning with renewed arousal and wanting more. Casting aside restraint, he fucked her furiously, her breasts jouncing, his fingers deep within her folds, agitating her clit mercilessly. She sobbed in her extremity, climaxing again as she felt him buck and come, emptying himself of seed.

They stood still, and she looked over his kingdom and wondered about his genes and what lurked in his DNA. Had his forebears been robber barons? It seemed more than likely. His penis slipped from her and she turned in his arms, seeing it still partially erect under the latex, the teat full of come. She was sorry when he removed the condom, knotted it and threw it over the edge, then replaced his cock in his black calf-skin trousers. He was composed once more, unsmiling as he kissed her slowly on the mouth.

'Time to go,' he said, taking his lips away and leaving her bereft. 'Philippe wants you downstairs in the stable and exercise yard.'

'The stable? But I can't ride,' she protested, trying to replace her thong and somehow eradicate the signs that she'd recently enjoyed coitus. It was impossible. Her cunt was too swollen and juicy. Philippe would be bound to notice.

'You'll not be expected to,' Damian returned, with a twinkle in his eye.

'Will he mind if he finds out you've been screwing me?' she asked, facing him full on. 'I wouldn't like to upset your precious deal.'

He seemed amused, even more confident and lordly strolling the battlements of his fortified house. Although the floor was strewn with dead leaves and feathers and fallen birds' nests, it didn't detract from

178

the grandeur. No one could be expected to keep towers tidy. As for the rest? It was like something out of a fairy-tale, and he the noble paladin about to rescue a fair damsel.

Herself? she thought as she climbed down the rickety stairs, clinging on for dear life. Not a chance. He had turned into the wicked sorcerer, selling his mistress to fulfil an ambition. Yet she didn't blame him, and couldn't think ill of him. I'm an idiot, she mused, her hand warm in his as he helped her down. As Shakespeare had once written, 'What fools these mortals be.'

There was no one about, the house fallen into an afternoon torpor while the sensible took a siesta. It rang with emptiness, and Judith imagined it to be bleak and haunted during the winter months. A caretaker looked after it, along with his wife, who was the housekeeper, and a head gardener. When the master came home, extra staff were taken on, mostly recruited from Mer. Down through the house they went, and along corridors, past splendid apartments that bewitched the senses and stunned the eye. She glimpsed a music room with a concert grand.

'Will you play for me?' she begged, lingering in the doorway. Light from the tall, narrow windows shimmered on the tiled floor; every floor was tiled there, bedrooms and all. 'So easy to keep clean,' Prunella had opined. It shone, too, on the closed lid of the black piano.

'I will, but for now you must concentrate on Philippe. I am more than merely delighted with the photograph. He must be made to feel that he didn't get the worst of the bargain.'

'Where are you keeping it?' she asked, wanting to prolong the moment, pained because he had released her hand.

'In a briefcase in my room. It's padlocked to the bed. I should put it away in the safe, I know, but am indulging myself, looking at it whenever I feel inclined. I've been after it for ten years, and the value has gone up annually.'

They had reached the ground floor and he took her outside and across a courtyard. The stable block had been constructed as part of the château, its façade a miracle of Renaissance architecture. It had huge, arched double doors to accommodate coaches drawn by a train of horses, and high windows through which poured rays of sunlight, grainy with dust and circling gnats. Judith's apprehension abated as they entered. It had a buoyant atmosphere.

'Once grooms, farriers, stable boys, and even a blacksmith with his forge and implements was employed, always ready to shoe my family's thoroughbreds. It's still busy. I pride myself on my bloodstock, and the services of my stallions are in constant demand. Look at this beauty,' Damian said, and took her across to a stall where stood a magnificent black beast, who snorted, tossed his noble head and rolled his eyes. Damian gentled him and he became quiet.

'You have a way with animals,' Judith said softly. 'Your dogs, your horses—'

'And my women,' he put in, mocking her as he fondled the stallion's mane and addressed him. 'Isn't that so, Crispin, my beauty? You know all about dealing with mares, mounting them firmly and nipping the backs of their necks as you plant your splendid seed deep within them.'

Crispin whinnied in reply and the noise attracted the attention of Philippe as he came in through a side door. He was dressed in beige riding breeches, a tweed jacket, a canary coloured waistcoat, brown boots and a brown bowler hat. He had a long whip with a plaited handle under one arm.

He addressed Judith gleefully. 'There you are, my dear.' He trailed his fingers down her cheek, adding, 'The air has done you good. You're all bright eyed and bushy tailed . . . or soon will be.' He rounded on his cadaverous valet, asking, 'Have you brought the outfit for Miss Shaw?'

'Yes, master,' Jay replied in a voice that could have belonged to either gender.

'I shall leave you,' Damian said, and patted Crispin for the final time.

It was useless longing to accompany him, and Judith accepted her lot. Only a few more days and she would be going home. She had never thought she'd miss Castleford, but she did, most definitely. She wanted to get back to work, to the job that she'd hardly begun to enjoy before being whisked away on outrageous adventures. Adam had promised to keep her post open and had reassured her that her wages would be paid regardless. It seemed that he had an arrangement with the Cresswells, and Judith could only speculate about their involvement.

Jay hung some articles over the side of a trestle and Judith stood still as the valet relieved her of the leather trappings and nipple clamps. The blood rushed into her tits, making them ruby-red. Philippe, seated on an upended barrel, drew in his breath between his teeth with a sharp hiss. The cool air of the stable gave her goose bumps and she was still unaccustomed to appearing in the nude. She waited, as nervous and highly-strung as Crispin, who was rustling in his stall, his hooves striking the straw-strewn cobbles.

The valet, deadpan and emotionless, fastened a

girth round Judith's waist. It was wide, covering her from ribs to pubis, and laced at the back like a corset. Jay clipped a crupper in place, passing it between her legs. It dug into her crack, pushing against her anus, its central strap stained by the moisture seeping from her sex. Despite the restraints, the fear and shame, Judith was throbbing with arousal. She could smell sex on her and worried that Philippe would be aware.

A gold studded collar was placed round her neck and buckled firmly. Her full breasts were emphasised by thongs passing underneath and lifting them, then criss-crossing over her chest. Philippe was almost hopping with excitement. He advanced upon her with another pair of nipple clamps, decorated with little silver bells.

Jay held her still while Philippe pressed the teeth open and then snapped them shut over her tormented teats. 'That's beautiful,' he cried, and slapped her breasts to make them shake. The bells tinkled.

She sat on a bench while Jay helped her into knee-high boots with wedged soles, lacing them tightly round her legs. Then cuffs were snapped on her wrists, her hair was teased out, and an elaborate head-dress fixed in place, glittering with gems and crested with white feathers. 'Get up,' said Jay, dragging at her arm.

She couldn't resist as a hand was thrust into her lower back, bending her over the trestle. Rigid with horror, she guessed what was going to happen next as the valet picked up a penis-shaped object with a long, flowing horsetail fixed to the base. She gripped the rim of the trestle and braced herself. Jay anointed the dildo's tip with oil, then spread her buttocks and inserted the end in her tight nether hole.

It was hard and it was large, but Anna had already

familiarised her with butt-plugs. Her muscles instinctively sought to reject it, but Jay was unrelenting. The slippery intruder penetrated deeper and deeper into her rectum. When she felt the tail tickle the backs of her thighs and experienced that full, strained feeling inside, she knew that she had been turned into the pony girl that Philippe desired.

He paced round her, smiling with delight and cracking the whip against the flagstones. 'Ah, you are so charming. I love that look. My own little filly who I can ride and punish and treat as I like.'

It was on the tip of Judith's tongue to remind him of animal rights, but she knew that this wry humour would elude him. She stood up and, head high like any equestrian circus performer, awaited his orders. Would he have her go down on hands and knees, crawling round while he got astride her back? She'd probably collapse under his weight. Oh, Damian, she raged in sudden anger, was this truly part of the bargain?

Jay led her through double doors at the rear of the stable into a covered exercise yard with a fence round the central arena. In keeping with the rest of the building, it reminded Judith of a renowned school, maybe in Vienna, where dressage had been taught for generations. It was deserted, but looked well maintained, as if it was often in use. Philippe stroked her tail as Jay went to a side bay and returned drawing a light, two-wheeled vehicle. It was a robust though elegant chariot, varnished in bottle green picked out in gold. She stared at it in puzzlement, until Jay backed her between the curved shafts and chained her to them by her wrist cuffs. Her fingers were free to grasp the wood.

'Open your mouth, sweetheart,' Philippe chortled

and, as she did so, he shoved a metal bit between her teeth. The bridle and reins were fastened to it by rings.

The bit was cold and hard. It forced her lips apart and made her want to gag. The dildo in her arse had its own particular ache, yet the thongs round her vulva stimulated her, lust rioting through her loins. The wedged boots made her feel club-footed and forced her to step high. She tossed her head, and the feathers shivered. Gingerly, she tested the balance of the little cart. She hardly felt it, for it was well constructed, a minor work of art designed especially for this purpose.

'Right, let's do it,' Philippe said, and Jay held Judith still while Philippe climbed into the cart and settled his large posterior on the velvet-covered seat and flourished his whip.

She was aware of the strain on her arms and the pull of the reins on the bit. The flick of the whip soon told her which way to turn, when to go and when to stop. Pain made her an apt pupil. With Jay leading her, she wheeled out into the arena, responding to the bridle's jerk. She was soon lathered in sweat, the whip keeping her at a steady trot, her back smarting, feet lifted high, tail swishing, the dildo stimulating her inner muscles until she was practically screaming for relief. They circumnavigated the exercise yard twice. Jay had left them now, and Philippe was controlling her.

He jerked on the reins. She stopped abruptly, saliva dripping from her mouth. The chariot bounced as he climbed down. Judith arched her aching back, then felt him behind her, and the emptiness as the dildo was removed from her fundament. But before she had time to gather her wits, he had replaced it with his cock.

'Glorious!' he muttered, moving faster in her arse-hole. 'My sweet little mare.'

He reached round, pushed aside the filly crupper and rubbed her clitoris. She panted with exertion and arousal, her clitoris thrumming under his rough handling. She needed to come so badly, half mad with the friction of straps rubbing her tender places, and the bouncing of her breasts that made the nipple clamps tighten and burn. The extreme pressure of Philippe's cock in her anus, the splitting sensation and the terrible driving need brought on her crisis. She convulsed between the shafts, orgasm exploding within her.

'That's it! Go for it!' Philippe yelled, giving a final jerk and leaning heavily against her back. 'Ah, you're worth every penny. Damian is welcome to *Mademoiselle Ninette*.'

Chapter 9

WHAT IS IT ABOUT the great outdoors that makes me horny? Kelly mused as Jake turned into a woody avenue where the trees met overhead and the Shogun's wheels jolted over ruts.

He'd offered to drive her around the estate. They'd had no further close contact since being in the château. There had been too many distractions – Anna, Peter, eating al fresco, idling by the swimming pool, every night a party night. The weather had turned warm, and there was the all-absorbing matter of acquiring a tan. Now there wasn't much time left, and her heart sank as she realised that she might never see him again.

The others were gearing themselves up for a pony race and, though the thought of being in command of a chariot or the prancing human steed pulling it thrilled her, she had accepted Jake's offer instead. They had driven through the grounds, and he had revealed his knowledge of the French Revolution and the damage done by the peasants to the great houses of the hated *aristos*.

'They were into destruction and looting, like any oppressed people who are suddenly top of the heap,' he said, one hand resting lightly on the wheel, the other arm along the Shogun's wound down window. Then he slowed as they came to a squat ruined tower. 'That was once a pigeonry. The aristocrats bred them as a delicacy for their tables, but the birds decimated the peasant's crops, leaving them on the verge of starvation. Naturally, when the power fell into their hands, the unlucky pigeons were the first to go.'

Kelly shivered, recalling lurid tales of that time – the guillotine and mob rule. She was glad when the forest closed about them, dark green and mysterious and isolated. It was as if they were the only couple alive in the world. The sense of intimacy was arousing, her juices wetting the seam of her panties, the chafing of her nipples against her crop top sending messages down to her clit. She sneaked a glance at Jake, admiring his craggy profile, his coppery skin and his firm jaw. She wanted to touch his arm, bared to the elbow and coated with a sprinkling of brown fuzz. She wanted him to kiss her, to feed on her mouth and nipples and slit. The thought sent shards of delight through her.

He smiled, though keeping his eyes on the rough track, and she had the feeling he knew what was running through her mind. Then he rolled the vehicle into a glade, braked and switched off the ignition. Taking his hand from the wheel, he put it on her knee, caressing her casually, going higher until his middle digit stroked across the crotch of her loose-fitting cotton pants.

Kelly sighed, opening her legs to the exquisite sensation, reaching out blindly and closing her hand over the prominent bulge at the front of his combats. He breathed deeply, thrusting against her palm and, at the same time, untying the drawstring of her pants and pushing them down around her belly. His fingers cruised lower, then combed through her russet wedge. He found her clit and massaged it firmly. Pleasure gushed through her and she came at once.

She nestled into his chest and he didn't withdraw his hand at once, cradling her pussy. Then he said firmly, '*Cher*, I'm going to fuck you.'

She was still convulsing and ready for anything, wanting his long tool inside her. He slid out of the driver's door and went round and opened hers, then drew her up to him and kissed her long and hard, before guiding her down an overgrown path and into a dell. She expected them to use the springy grass as a bed, but Jake thrust her up against a tree, the bark digging into her bare spine. He wasn't in the mood for teasing now, his face dark and intense with all the passion of a red-blooded male who lusts to bury his cock in a warm, wet orifice. His hands were under her top, pushing it up like a band round her chest, baring her nipples to his touch. His mouth was marvellous, tasting her lips, her tongue and her tits.

Then her trousers were down round her ankles and she stepped out of them. Her knickers followed. His khaki combats were open and his cock was out, and he lifted her and impaled her on it. She gave a little shriek of satisfaction as it penetrated deeply, folding her legs round his waist and clinging to him to give him greater purchase. He grunted, working his pelvis in a steady motion that brought him closer to orgasm. The bark scraped her back as he slid her up and down the length of his shaft, and she moaned each time the cock-ring reached her ultimate depth. His hand was between them, thumb-pad rotating on her clitoris, and crazy jolts of pleasure crackled through her loins as she came again.

She wanted to lose herself in him, opening her eyes to see the dense canopy of foliage over their heads and the sun-flecked bower that was her own personal Eden. She feared that she was about to sacrifice her independence to this man. What price girl-power compared with surrender to him? She stroked his untidy brown hair and gripped his muscular shoulders as he fucked her savagely, reaching his own completion.

'Jeez, honey, that sure was something, huh?' he murmured into her hair.

His penis slipped out of her, and he gently lowered her until her feet touched the ground. Then he released her and zipped up his trousers. He didn't say anything further until he had heaved a wicker hamper from the back of the Shogun. He carried it across to a smooth flat area, opened it and proceeded to spread out a superb picnic.

'Hey, where did you get this?' she asked, flopping down on the grass and leaning her cheek against his shoulder. She knew this to be a girlish, my-man's-wonderful gesture, but didn't care.

'Sweet-talked the housekeeper, who had a word with the chef,' he said, grinning unrepentantly.

'Talk about the gift of the gab,' she exclaimed, pulling herself together and controlling her desire to be soppy.

They ate in companionable silence, sampling the superb cuisine. There was even a bottle of sparkling white wine. 'A vintage brew from Damian's cellar,' Jake announced. 'Here's mud in your eye.' Then he rested back on his elbows, squinted across at her and added, 'I'm off to Blois. You coming?'

'I could, I suppose,' she said, thinking: try and stop me, mate.

'I'm going to see a buddy of mine who is a whiz at fakes,' he continued, shading his eyes against the filtered sunshine.

Kelly grew still, sipping her wine and wondering about him. 'Why are you doing that?' she asked slowly.

'Because, sugar-baby, I've just stolen Damian's prize photo,' he replied.

Her heart skipped a beat and then sped on. 'You've what?' she gasped.

'Acquired *Mademoiselle Ninette* illegally,' he replied as calmly as if they were discussing the weather. 'Well, not quite that. I'd better explain. What I'm doing is fulfilling a contract.'

'I don't get it,' she said, wrestling with a host of unpleasant connotations, not least of which was the possibility of the sack from her job in the bookshop should Damian think she was any way implicated.

'Listen up, Kelly, and listen good,' Jake said with a laugh, sitting now, his arms resting on his raised knees. 'Dealing can be a dirty business. The photograph was stolen from a New Orleans family who had it in their possession for years. In fact, Ninette was a great-great-great-grandmother, somewhere along the line. Yep, she went out there, married, turned respectable and ran a thrift store. This later became big business and she died rich. She kept the sexy picture of herself under wraps. It was secretly passed down from father to son, then it vanished. Recently they hired me to do a search. I traced it to France.'

Kelly didn't know whether to believe him or not. Was he a con man? 'You've just stolen it. How did you do that? Judith told me Damian had it in a briefcase locked up in his bedroom.'

'He did.'

'Then how did you get your thieving paws on it?'

He tapped the side of his nose. 'It's down to the power of the dollar. All men are venal, or hadn't you noticed? Women, too.'

'You used bribery,' she accused. 'How dirty can you get?'

'You ain't seen nothing yet. Are you trying to tell me that Damian didn't know it was hot? My sources prove that Philippe Laveau certainly did.'

'He made no secret of owning it. No, I don't think Damian knew.'

'What makes you think he's Mr Perfect?'

'I don't, but I doubt he'd want to get mixed up in anything shady. Give it back to him right away.'

'You've got to be kidding. I've promised the rightful owners. Besides, they've paid me mega bucks to find it, and more when it's delivered.'

'You're a skunk!' she shouted. 'A double-dealing bastard! Do you ever do anything unless there's something in it for you?'

'Hush now, Kelly. Can't you see that the whole set-up is crazy? Laveau gets a hold of it, then he sells it to Damian, but my clients are the legal owners. Sure, I get money out of it. I'm not a charity organisation. My buddy is the best there is. He'll make a copy like you've never seen. I'll return it before Damian finds out it's gone and he won't be any the wiser. Everyone will be happy, including me with my wad.'

'Is that the reason you went to Philippe's cocktail party and spoke to me? Was there nothing else?' she asked, tears stinging her eyes.

'There wasn't, until I got to know you, then things changed. I still had a job to do, but now there was you.'

'What about Anna?'

'Anna and me are past history. But I've a feeling *we*

can make it together. I saw this mambo priestess before I left New Orleans and she told me I was going to meet someone very special.'

'What the hell's that . . . a mambo priestess?' Kelly was fighting to maintain her anger and indignation, but it was melting away, warmed by his eyes and his smile.

'A voodoo practitioner. Don't knock it. It's a very old, very strong belief, a kind of cross between African religions and Roman Catholicism. A lot of folk follow it, and I'm no exception when I want a lucky spell, or need to look into the future. And I think she was right. I've met that special person. You.'

'What crap!' she said, yet desperately wanted to believe he was sincere. 'Have you ever kissed the Blarney Stone?'

'Nope, but some of my ancestors came over from Ireland,' he admitted, then put his arm round her and added persuasively, 'You coming to Blois? We can leave the picture with Dean, that's my buddy, bum around the town for a while and pick it up later. Damian won't miss it tonight. They're having a shindig after the race so everyone will be partying.'

'I'm not sure. It isn't just the money. Judith allowed herself to be used.'

'I feel bad about that. Laveau's a creep.'

'Don't feel too bad. I guess she's enjoyed some of it, and she wanted to please Damian.'

'OK then. Let's go.' He was on his feet and pulling her up.

'Where's the photo?'

'In the car.'

'I think you'd better take me back to the château.'

'Why?' He looked genuinely disappointed.

'Because I don't want any part of it.'

'But you were to be my alibi. And it's not only that. I like being with you, Kelly.'

'Take me back. I've some thinking to do. I don't know if I can trust you again.'

His hand was tender on her cheek and she wished she wasn't so cynical and hard-boiled. It would have been great to see him as some modern-day knight-errant, galloping around righting wrongs.

'If that's what you really want?' he said.

'It is . . . just for today,' she answered.

Kelly found everyone in the stable. She was feeling guilty and cursing Jake for burdening her with his secret. He had been right about the pony cart racing. She was just in time to see the start.

Anna was stupendous, dressed as an Amazon queen, encased in light armour, her breasts bare, her nipples rouged. She wore a tiny white pleated kilt that barely reached her fork, her naked mound showing with every movement. Metal arm-bands, sandal-boots buckled from ankle to knee, and a brass helmet flaunting ostrich feathers completed her costume. Peter, stripped of everything save harness, was chained to her black chariot. She was in position with her legs planted firmly, the reins in one hand and a whip in the other. She flicked this over his haunches, commanding that he endure the sting without flinching.

Kelly saw Judith, near-naked and with a tail thrust into her anus, strapped to Philippe's carriage. He was tugging on the bit, forcing Judith to keep her head high. Several other guests were attired as charioteers or huntsmen and their steeds waited impatiently for the signal. These were slaves, handsome young men with thongs round their cocks, keeping them erect, and beautiful girls wearing basques and no panties, their nipples and clits stained red, matching the stripes laid on by their masters' or mistresses' whips.

Damian wore a ringmaster's regalia, with white breeches, a red coat, black boots and a top hat. Prunella was his pony for the day. She looked at ease in the straps that bound her to his cart. She tossed her mane and waggled the tail in her rump. Fadil, as umpire, raised a snowy handkerchief and let it drop. The pony carts bowled into action.

The competition was keen. The participants and spectators had placed bets on the outcome. Kelly was glad that they were so enthusiastic; at least it would occupy Damian for hours to come. She made certain that she was available should they decide on further heats. She'd never been a pony girl but had heard about clubs where weekenders went to become handlers or spirited horses. It appealed to subs and doms alike, each achieving their own particular satisfaction.

One of the fillies dropped out with a sprained ankle and Kelly took her place. It was rather like playing at horses as a child. She was stripped, then buckled and laced into the trappings. It felt real, as if she actually was a frisky mare. She stamped the cobbles in her high boots, tossed her mane and neighed. She even lashed out at her groom, catching him in the balls, but was whipped into line by her handler, a statuesque lesbian friend of Anna's, called Brenda.

There were other treats in store for later. Damian had opened his dungeons to the chosen few. The tackle was removed and the ponies hosed down. Kelly needed this badly, stinking of sweat and leather, her rump stinging from Brenda's over-zealous leathering. But all in all, it had been invigorating, far better than a stint of aerobics or kickboxing. She grabbed the chance to speak with Judith as they towelled themselves dry in the tack room.

'Are you OK?' she asked, for Judith's backside bore vivid marks laid on top of purple bruises.

'Yes. Are you?' Judith replied absentmindedly, and Kelly noticed that her eyes were on Damian, where he leaned against a stall, murmuring to a coal-black stallion.

Damn! Kelly thought. Judith's still besotted. She suddenly wanted to go home, tired of this self-indulgent, decadent crowd. Most of all, she wanted to see Jake, but not yet. The best help she could give him was to distract Damian for as long as possible.

The staff had prepared an after-race buffet, ignoring the shenanigans in the exercise yard. The Great Hall resounded with talk and laughter as the champagne flowed. Some had changed into fresh animal trappings, others wore hunting rig, and there was a preponderance of corsets and suspenders, bare breasts and exposed cunts. Anna had donned a gold lamé sheath dress that fitted her body as if moulded on her. It was sleeveless, had a deep cleavage, and the back was practically non-existent, cut so low that the top of her bottom crease showed. Kelly, not to be outdone, had put on a short red satin skirt, no knickers, and a diaphanous blouse that displayed her scarlet lace bra. Judith was still a pony, led around by a halter gripped in Philippe's chubby fist.

As the sky darkened and the full moon rode high attended by a retinue of stars, any kow-towing to accepted social behaviour went by the board. High jinks led to games of a sexual nature where handlers mounted their steeds, and couples were having sex, or were joined by a third, even a fourth person, their

195

gender of no importance. Exotic music mingled with the laughter and the moans of pleasure – the sensual notes of guitars, the throb of drums.

Peter came rushing across to Kelly, absurd in his curly wig and Fifi dress. 'Anna's taking me to the dungeon,' he said. 'I'm to be rewarded for winning the final heat today.'

Kelly was already familiar with that gloomy place. Anna had not been slow in introducing her to it. It was far more impressive than the tacky basements of several fetish clubs she had visited in London. It had to be. It was the real thing.

She passed through a small door concealed by a tapestry, and went along a narrow, dimly lit passageway. She could hear Peter breathing excitedly. It was almost comical, the way he had taken to masochism like a duck to water.

They went down some steps and emerged into a room where the arched roof was upheld by columns. It was cool there, despite the fire roaring up the chimney. There were several people lolling on couches, watching Judith, who was tied to a crosspiece, her face pressed against the upright, her arms roped and pulled above her head, her ankles tethered to rings set in the floor. Philippe was beating her, the blows echoing through the dungeon. When he tired momentarily, the hatchet-faced Jay took over.

Torchlight flickered across Judith's face and her eyes were closed and her head strained back, her mouth emitting sounds that could have indicated agony or extreme ecstasy. The spectators were silent, but the sight was making them restless. They groped their genitals, or those of the person nearest to them, rapt expressions on their faces as they stared at Judith.

'You're a bad slave-slut,' Philippe shouted, shoving Jay aside and belabouring Judith with a flexible paddle. 'We lost, due to your dawdling. I don't like losing, and it's cost me money.'

'Oh, please, master. Be merciful,' she moaned, and turned her face to one side against the harsh surface of the wood. She wasn't appealing to Philippe, but to Damian.

He stepped closer, snarling at Philippe, 'It appears to me that you haven't yet learned the difference between using a slave and giving her the chance to benefit from the experience. Don't forget that she's still a novice. I suggest that you submit to Madam Anna. She's an excellent teacher.'

'She is, she is,' cried Peter, and flung himself at Anna's feet, clawing at her legs and wailing, 'My reward, mistress. You promised.'

She shook him off and he lay sprawled on the stone flags, his cheek resting on her foot. She dragged herself free and stabbed at him with her stiletto heel. 'How dare you demand anything of me?' she hissed. 'Up with your skirt, you tart!'

Peter couldn't wait. He bent over, his arse lifted, his thighs planted firmly as he awaited her first swipe. It was fierce and noisy. She lifted her arm again, the cane whistling as it fell for a second time. Philippe was intrigued by the sight, creeping closer, and Kelly saw Damian approach Judith, and the devotion in her friend's tear-filled eyes as he coasted over her fiery rump and let his fingers enter her divide.

Kelly was feeling uncomfortably randy. The very air seemed to crackle with pheromones. But no one took any notice of her and she felt disgruntled. Then Brenda sidled up to her, slipped a hand under Kelly's mini-skirt and patted her bare bottom. Kelly leaned into those pats and caresses, longing for the dextrous fingers to locate her clit.

'I can feel the welts my whip left on your butt,' Brenda whispered, her breath stirring strands of Kelly's hair. 'You did good. We got a second. Damian will present the cups later on tonight.'

Her other arm came round Kelly, cradling her breasts under the transparent blouse, and pinching the tips of her nipples. Kelly lifted her mons towards Brenda's fingers, a long sigh escaping the girl's lips as she inserted two into Kelly's wet vulva and wriggled them expertly. Brenda knew what she wanted, keeping her fingers inside, but circling Kelly's clitoris with her thumb, caressing it on each side, drawing back the little cowl and tickling the sensitive head.

Anna abandoned Peter and she and Prunella fell upon Philippe, taking off his clothes while he protested weakly. The state of his cock confirmed that he was more than ready for anything they might choose to do. They stretched him on his back on a padded bench, deftly imprisoned his wrists and ankles, then paraded about in front of him, displaying their cunts. Anna lifted her gold dress and straddled him, bending her knees and brushing his straining weapon with the outer edge of her labia. He jerked upwards, but she lifted her leg and stepped aside gracefully.

'No, not yet, you naughty boy,' she chided, and picked up the pliable paddle he'd been using on Judith. It was covered in white leather and twanged when she bent it and then let it go. She swung her arm and brought the paddle down across Philippe's fat thighs.

He yelped, but his cock swelled even more and he suddenly ejaculated, spurting a stream of milky semen

198

that landed on his obese belly and flabby chest. Anna shook her head and ranted at him. 'Disgraceful! Where's your control? I can see I'm going to have to be very strict with you. No more games with Judith. You'll be dealing with me from now on.' And she changed the paddle for a flogger.

Kelly was aware of them, and aware, too, of Damian releasing Judith from her bondage, taking her in his arms and kissing her, then a tidal wave of bliss crashed over her and she came against Brenda's hand. It took a second for the world to right itself. When it did, she looked across the vault and found herself staring into Jake's keen blue eyes. He winked and gave her the thumbs up.

She wasn't sure if this meant he approved of her going with a dyke, or that his mission had been successful.

'And you'll only have the men I choose,' Judith heard Damian say as she lay blindfolded and bound hand and foot by silken scarves to the four-poster bed. 'You didn't warm to that horrible little reptile, Philippe, did you? Didn't enjoy him sticking his fat cock in you?'

'No, master,' she averred, aware of him bending over her – smelling him, hearing him, her other senses sharpened because he had denied her her sight.

When he had taken her to the Master Chamber she had felt nothing but intense relief. Philippe had been left to Anna's tender mercies and Damian had seemed anxious to be alone with Judith. As if to re-establish possession of her, he'd tied her and covered her eyes. With lax limbs and a sense of blissful enjoyment, she had felt him rubbing balm into her bruises, and this had been followed by other sensations as he touched her breasts and cleft with something as soft as rabbit's fur. Just as she was responding to the sensual feel of it, he had dripped melting ice-cubes over her nipples, making her yell. Then his mouth warmed her teats, sucking and arousing until she was at screaming pitch.

Trapped in velvety darkness, adrenalin pumping, she moaned and strained at her wrist bands as he slowly, slowly, traversed her belly, her bare pubis, the arrow of hair, until his tongue darted between her folds and found her clitoris. He spread her thighs as far as the scarves would permit, and then he was between them, his breath hot on her nooks and crannies as he stretched open her labia, pinched her clit in his fingers and applied his tongue to the swollen head.

Sensation gathered in her womb, connecting with her spine, her thighs, the tips of her toes. Damian sucked and flicked his tongue over the tiny, tormented bud, and every nerve in Judith's body responded. She tossed her head from side to side, pressed her pelvis high against his mouth, and the rushing, dizzying force of orgasm took her and shook her and tossed her high among the stars.

As she dallied there, before starting the slow descent to normality, she felt his cock at her entrance and the strong thrust of his hips driving it home. He pushed his hands under her buttocks, holding her to him, and now there was no further delay as he took his pleasure fiercely.

He didn't withdraw from her immediately, but rolled to one side and lay there for a while, his breathing slowing, his hand stroking her hair. Then she felt the mattress sag as he knelt and untied her restraints. His fingers were at the back of her head, undoing the knot, and she blinked as her eyes became accustomed to the candlelight.

He pulled the duvet over them and hauled her into his arms, her head pillowed on his shoulder. She was astonished into silence by this unusually tender gesture.

'We're leaving tomorrow,' he said. 'Driving to Paris and boarding Eurostar. I've got what I came for, and want to head for the Rectory.'

'Taking *Mademoiselle Ninette* home,' she said, filled with an aching joy. It was so sweet to have him there beside her. Maybe he'd stay all night as she had always longed for him to do.

'Yes. Would you like to see her again?' he asked, his mood soft and amiable. He reached under the bed and pulled out a briefcase. In an instant he had unlocked it and drawn out a folder, opening it for her inspection. 'There she is, in all her brazen glory,' he said, gloating over his prize.

'Will you display her at the Rectory?' she asked, gazing down at the brown and white photograph, so well preserved after one hundred and fifty years.

He looked from Ninette to Judith as if comparing them, and finding the two of them delightful. 'I shall keep it locked away, only bringing it out on special occasions. Just to know that it's in my possession will be enough.' He put down the photo and lifted Judith's hand to his lips, astounding her by adding, 'Thank you for helping me get it.'

Kelly leaned on the Shogun, saying goodbye to Jake. It was early, the white mist drifting over the water meadows presaging another hot day. There were other vehicles outside the château, rapidly filling up with passengers and baggage.

'Don't go back to England. Come with me,' Jake said, yet again.

'And where might that be?' she asked. He was so hard to resist.

'America. I've a delivery to make, remember?' he teased, his smiling eyes crinkled at the outer corners. He was looking remarkably sexy, in cut-offs and terrain sandals, alluring her with his devil-may-care attitude.

'I do. You're a lucky bastard to have got away with it,' she managed to say.

'I told you Dean was the greatest faker out. His stuff should be hung in galleries. We'd have known by now if Damian suspected.' He put his arm round her waist, and she was terribly conscious of his masculine attraction. Her pussy clenched and she wanted him so badly, nearly capitulating as he insisted, 'Come to the States with me. What have you got to lose?'

'One hell of a lot,' she said, pulling away from his embrace.

'Oh, babe, you don't know what you're missing. I can offer you a flesh-fest and wall-to-wall sunshine. OK, you won't come now, but I'll be phoning you until you do.'

He grabbed her again and walked her round to the far side of the Shogun where it was parked close to a high hedge. There he pushed her against it, lifted her skirt, dragged her tanga to one side and, with one sure stroke, impaled her on his cock.

The shock of it rendered her speechless, then, 'Jake!' she squealed, while her insides melted at the feel of that firm hot tool. 'For God's sake! Someone may see!'

'I don't give a fuck. Do you?'

She found that she didn't. In fact, the idea of being watched while she fornicated with him was stimulating. I'm turning into an exhibitionist! she thought, while it was possible to think at all. It'll be strip-joints next, showing off my pussy and earning buckets of cash.

His face blocked out the sky. His mouth descended on hers, his tongue sliding between her teeth. He thrust it in and out, echoing the movement of his cock poking harshly into her. Sensations trembled through her, but she knew she wouldn't come unless he rubbed her clit. He opened her blouse and tweaked her nipples through her bra, then found the front fastening and clicked it open. The two halves fell apart and she lifted her breasts towards his fingers. He flicked her nipples into sharper points, still working his penis in and out.

Suddenly he pulled it out and flipped her over, pulling down her panties and baring her buttocks. She could feel his cock driving into the deep crease between them, sliding past her arsehole and burrowing into her vagina. The exterior of the Shogun was slippery and she clung to the frame for support, taking the full force of Jake's penetration. She felt his hand under her, fingers combing her bush, and landing on her throbbing bud. The rough, arousing strokes sent tremors through her.

'Do it harder! Yes, yes!' she urged. There was no time for gentle fondling now. 'Oh, Jake . . . make me come.'

'Jeez!' he muttered, massaging her so hard that she wasn't sure if she was feeling pain or the ultimate pleasure. He was pumping furiously, making the sturdy FWD shake.

'Now, now . . .' she whimpered as her orgasm swelled.

'Yes, baby . . . now,' he repeated hoarsely, his finger matching the speed of his thrusts.

Now she had it, that hot, compelling sensation

gathering force and sweeping her to a crisis so intense that she sobbed as it peaked.

With a pounding heart, she was aware of a chill as he pulled out. Immediately conscious, too, of where they were and the inappropriate nature of their action, she hurriedly adjusted her underclothes and outer garments.

She looked across the gravelled drive, where there were cars and people, but no one seemed to have noticed what they had been doing. Jake grinned at her, and she could feel her resolutions dissolving, but, 'This doesn't make any difference,' she said. 'I'm still not coming to America.'

'But—'

'No buts,' she continued, having to look away from him. There was no way she was going to become a victim again, ever.

It had always been her lot to fall for the bad boys, the charming, feckless rogues, but never again. As she'd told Judith, she'd been there, done that and had the T-shirt to prove it. Love wasn't for her.

Chapter 10

ADAM HAD LEFT JUDITH in charge of the shop while he went out. She was used to this now, answering the phone, coping with customers, ordering items and using the Internet. He had bought another computer, fixed it up behind the counter and paid for her to have lessons.

Two months had passed since that strange time at the château. Adam had welcomed her home with open arms, and she had settled down happily, finding herself ever more confident. They had become close, not exactly an item, Damian wouldn't have countenanced that, but liking each other's company. Adam had taken her to concerts, the opera and the ballet, and introduced her to a variety of exotic dishes, something of a gourmet. He also made love to her sometimes, and took part in scenes at the Rectory.

But Damian was the greatest influence in her life. He had taught her that it was possible to obtain relief from anxiety by transferring the fight–flight impulses into sexual ones. She had learned to accept pain, elevating it to the emotional and physical exhaustion of a passionate love affair. He had explained that it was all down to wanting to win the love and approval of her master. She had told him about her feelings of inadequacy as a child; her parents only showing real concern if she was ill or injured.

He chastised her, and brought her to the peak of passion. He educated her in other ways – politics, the arts, world affairs – and treated her to piano recitals as an aperitif to sex and punishment.

Now she was a far cry from the shy thing that had applied to Adam for a job. Her self-esteem had shot up. She had faced fear and humiliation and not only survived, but been rewarded with orgasms and love. When she tried to talk this over with Kelly, her friend dismissed it as psychobabble, advising Judith to enjoy it and ignore the analysis bit. She'd taken her advice, but found that Damian's theories had rubbed off on her anyway. The change had been subtle but sure. She'd had her mousy hair highlighted and dressed in a French pleat. Contact lenses had replaced her glasses, and she wore chic clothes to work, but went wild when in the company of her lovers.

She smiled as her fingers touched the keypads. Yes, she could think of them in the plural, Adam and Damian, but then, of course, there was icing on the cake: her relationships with Anna and Kelly. She must be the luckiest person alive.

As if conjured up by her thoughts, Kelly poked her head round the door of the inner office, her mass of teased and streaked chestnut hair like something out of a fantasy movie. 'You running the lab this morning?' she joked.

'I don't think so. Just Adam's stooge.'

'How about a cup of coffee and a cream cake?' Kelly suggested.

'Good idea,' Judith answered, clicking the mouse

and logging on to a worldwide web for books. Almost any title under the sun could be ordered there.

'Guess what I've done,' Kelly said, bringing in two mugs of instant coffee and a plate of sticky confectionery.

Judith pressed Save and sat back in her operator's chair. It was nearly lunchtime and the morning rush had subsided. 'I don't know – got a date with Russell Crowe?' she said, getting a quick flash of him fighting for his life in the gladiatorial games.

'Nope, though I wouldn't say no,' Kelly grinned, sitting on a corner of the desk and swinging her bare, brown legs, gold toe-nails glinting in sandals with platform soles.

'Are those new?' Judith was sure they were. Sharing the cottage and driving around in Tracy gave them little privacy. They practically lived in each other's pockets. It was a tad irksome at times. 'And why are you wearing platforms?' she added, a touch acidly.

'Because I can,' Kelly retorted, but she wasn't cross and seemed to be full of news she was dying to impart.

'OK, so what have you been up to?' Judith asked.

'I phoned my mother. Yes, I know I've put it off for months, but I thought – what the hell. Jesus, she sounded almost obscenely happy.'

'That's not surprising. She's carrying her lover's child, isn't she?'

'I went all squidgy on her,' Kelly confessed. 'I wished her and the sprog well and she cried down the phone, said she was so glad I'd rung. I don't know what's come over me, but I've been looking at teddy bears and little clothes in Baby Gap, thinking of buying a present for my brother or sister, when it arrives.'

'I like it,' Judith said, aware of a lump in her throat.

'You do?' Kelly seemed puzzled by her own behaviour.

'Yes, and I'd like to send a card or something when she's given birth.'

'God, we're turning into a right pair of sloppy jerks,' Kelly said scornfully, but it was obvious she was pleased underneath.

'Maybe we're just growing up.'

'Fuck! I hope not,' Kelly said. 'That smacks of responsibility. To change the subject . . . Alden Ray left an e-mail. He does it from time to time. Anyway, he's playing Glastonbury and says he wants me to go with him – he'll get me a pass for free. We've got this sometimes thing going.'

'What about Jake?'

'Him too. He's always phoning or leaving notes at my Net address. So what? I can do with more than one cock in my life. You've got at least two, and what's happened between you and Peter?' Kelly sounded a little aggrieved.

Judith was aware that Jake had got to her friend. She refused to discuss him, which wasn't like Kelly at all. She was usually communicative about her men. Judith had the distinct feeling that something traumatic had taken place in France, but though she racked her brains, she couldn't for the life of her come up with a solution.

'Peter asked me to marry him, but I said no,' she answered. 'I don't want to settle down as his wife and raise a family. He's sweet and I'll always have a soft spot for him, but I like him much better now that he's a transvestite. He's bought himself a house so that he can launder his frilly underwear and hang his frocks in the wardrobe without his mother asking awkward questions.'

The shop door opened and Adam came in. 'All right, girls?' he asked, and went over to Judith, kissing her fondly on the lips.

'Hey, I'm out of here. Got a rock star to mail. See you later,' Kelly said, and darted out to the back of the shop.

'Shall we go upstairs?' Adam asked, locking the shop door.

She couldn't refuse his lazy smile, his hesitancy that covered an above average brain, his good looks and rumpled clothing, all of which smacked of the absent-minded professor. But he was far from that; she'd seen him with Anna, becoming her slave, and joining in any unusual games she might think up. Judith had forgiven him for luring her into the Cresswell's web. In fact it had been the making of her. Without it she might still have been the sad person who found her release in dreams.

She loved Adam's apartment over the shop, her heart thumping as she preceded him up the stairs, anticipating a session in his bed. He had left the windows open, and the white net curtains stirred in the light breeze. It was a hot day, approaching midsummer, and she stepped on to the wide balcony and sighed as she sank down on a lounger facing the garden. It was a suntrap, and she took off her jacket, then her blouse, bared to the burgundy silk and lace bra. Adam appeared with two glasses of lemonade, tinkling with ice. He had taken off his shirt, swirls of dark hair obscuring his pecs and nut-brown nipples. He placed the drinks on a side table and leaned over to kiss her. He was very good at kissing, tangling his tongue with hers, and pulling away before it got boring and routine.

Then he took the reclining chair beside her and

turned his face to the sun, eyes shaded by dark glasses. 'You've taken to bookselling like a natural,' he said. 'I want you to take an even larger part. I think you're ready to go to an auction sale and perhaps a book fair without me.'

Pleasure bubbled up in her. He was trusting her to make important decisions. At one time she would have been scared to death, but now, 'I'd like that. You've already taught me so much about the trade. I'm sure I can cope.'

'I'm sure you can, too,' he said, and yawned sleepily. 'A catnap, I think, and then we're going to the Rectory. It's early closing day, remember? And we deserve a treat. Damian and Anna are expecting us. Take off your clothes, my dear. You'll get unsightly strap marks.'

She did so, and then, regretfully accepting that he wasn't about to make love to her, she soaked up the sunshine, while inside her desire mounted – a tingling frustration that Damian had trained her to endure.

When she finally arrived at the Rectory, her breasts were sore with wanting, her nipples like red-hot coals and her clit swollen and throbbing.

Fadil led them towards the gymnasium, where the clash of steel and the stamping of feet indicated that Damian was in the middle of a fencing lesson. In his mask, padded jacket and coarse linen breeches, he was everything that Judith could have wished for in a handsome hero. He and his opponent didn't stop their bout as Judith and Adam entered. They lunged, parried and performed the graceful riposte, then Damian appeared to slip, his left hand on the ground . . . a thrust upwards and he was under his fencing master's guard, the point of his foil at his throat. He straightened up and they bowed courteously, the contest over.

Damian strolled over to Judith, pulling off his gauntlets before removing his mask. Sweat streamed down his face from his tangled black hair. She could smell his musky odour and her pussy spasmed, the lust she had repressed throughout the afternoon gathering inside her like a tidal wave. He took off his jacket and towelled over his chest and armpits. He had a perfect body, wide shoulders tapering to a narrow waist, a flat belly where a squiggle of dark hair disappeared into his waistband. The breeches were tight, and she saw the line of his cock pressed against his inner thigh.

He smiled and touched her cheek. 'Join me in the bath, slave,' he ordered, then glanced at Adam. 'You too. Anna is waiting there for us. We're ready to hear your confession. I'm sure you've sinned and need correction.'

Judith's heart raced as she pictured the dungeon, and she obeyed, as much the mistress as the slave these days. She had found the freedom to express herself any way she wanted. She leaned against Damian, thinking about the kiss of the lash, the embrace of chains and the oblivion of the blindfold. Whenever she shared carnal experiences with anyone else it would be orchestrated by Damian. He was her master for all time.

Kelly invited Caroline and Sally to go with her to Glastonbury. She'd rather outgrown them, and had the gut feeling that this would be the last outing together. She drove to Bristol and there met up with the band, leaving the girls to fuck away to their heart's content as they travelled down to Somerset in a coach with blacked-out windows, the interior designed for comfort. Kelly preferred to drive Tracy. With her knowledge of the car's internal workings, she had no fears about breaking down. She loathed the idea of being dependent on someone else for transport, and could now leave at any given second, provided the traffic conditions would allow.

Right now these looked bleak, the roads to the festival jam-packed with fans heading for the three-day event. Parking was provided for the band and camp followers. There was a modest caravan for the musicians and a super luxurious one for Alden Ray. Gazing from one of the windows as the light started to fade, Kelly was glad she wasn't camping out there amidst the thousands of people setting up their tents and hoping it would stop raining and that they wouldn't get ripped off or arrested. There was a substantial police presence. The queues for the Portaloos were depressingly long, the standpipes already awash with mud. I'm getting too old for roughing it, she decided. I don't want to get all mucky. I'm used to having money now, and a good job, and as much S&M as I can handle.

'I'm on stage in half an hour,' Alden said, the man she had thought godlike a few months ago. Now he was just a bolshie, overconfident, brash male who was pushing his cock slowly in and out of her pussy.

In honour of the occasion she was garbed in leather – a short black skirt and a bustier, high boots with thick soles, her mascara heavy, and her hair spiked and gelled.

They had been on the bed, his tongue paddling over her nipples, his fingers palpating her clit so that she was racked with tiny spasms. Then he had knelt across her, yanked off her panties and rammed his hard, curved cock into her wet snatch again. She reached between their pounding hips and rubbed her button, the culmination of sensation in clit and cunt providing the stimulation she needed. She let go, her body shaking as she climaxed.

Alden grabbed her buttocks, lifting her to him, and pumping away like fury until he suddenly grunted and came into the condom.

Someone hammered on the caravan door, shouting, 'Five minutes and we're on, Alden!'

He heaved himself off her, wiped his penis and zipped up his jeans, then glanced in the mirror to see that he hadn't smeared his make-up. 'See you after the show,' he said. 'Be there for me, or else I just might have to screw someone else,' he threatened, and he picked up his guitar and left.

'Get stuffed,' Kelly muttered under her breath.

She felt stale and used. She'd used Alden as much as he'd used her, of course, but there was a foul taste to it all. She heard the roar of the crowd as the StingRayz erupted on to the central pyramid stage. It was the same kind of roar that had greeted gladiatorial games. An animal roar that demanded sweat, blood and tears. Nothing had changed.

She stepped into her panties, tidied herself, picked up her bag and left. OK, so it might take her hours to get through the traffic and reach Castleford, but it didn't matter. She had some serious thinking to do.

Kelly tucked Tracy up in the garage, then turned the key in the cottage door. At first, seeing lights in the living room, she thought Judith was home, then gave a little shriek of astonished delight as Jake swept her into his arms.

'When did you get here? Why didn't you let me know to expect you?' she shouted, pummelling his shoulders and relishing the wonderful feel and smell of him, yet feeling a little guilty because her pussy was still wet from Alden.

'Just couldn't stay away any longer, and I figured if I hopped on a plane I'd be here almost as fast as mailing you.'

'Oh, Jake, I'm so glad you did. I was just going to call you. I've been to a rock festival but it's not for me any more. I might even hook into the classics Judith raves about.'

'You? I don't believe it, *cher*. What's brought this on?'

'I don't know. Maybe I'm getting past it,' she said, finding it impossible to think straight while he was petting her breasts and running his hands soothingly over her back and down to her buttocks.

'Not you. You need a change of scene. Why don't you come back to America with me?'

'I've a job to do,' she reminded him, though the cottage parlour looked so right with his kit-bag and ski-jacket lying around.

'Haven't you a vacation due?' he asked, running his tongue tip round the lobe of her ear and setting her earring swinging.

'I have,' she said, thinking: I can do it. I want to do it. Maybe I won't come back. I'll leave the cottage and Tracy in Judith's care. Then an unpleasant thought popped into her mind. 'What about *Mademoiselle Ninette*?' She'd not dared speak of it over the phone or Internet.

'Safe back home with its tightful owners. Has Damian ever mentioned it?'

'No. He gets it out sometimes when he wants to have a gloat, and seems unaware of the swap.'

'I told you Dean was a star, didn't I? Now will you stop worrying and fuck me?'

214

Kelly followed both instructions, and it was heart-warming to take him to her bedroom, where the ceiling was supported by age-old black beams and her bed was wide and covered with a patchwork quilt.

Here his patience ran out, and so did hers. It had been months since they had shared intimacy, and their clothes were soon scattered on the floor. She flung back the duvet and they dived into bed, snuggling close, almost clumsy with haste. It felt so right to be there with him, and she wound her legs round his sleek hips and drew him closer to the centre of her being. There was no awkwardness or hesitation. They came together as if two halves of the same being, his cock and the Prince Albert penetrating her, his mouth on hers, his hands on her breasts. And when she wriggled a little, letting him know that her clit was feeling ignored, he stopped seeking his own satisfaction and made sure she achieved hers.

Later, they lay curled up like two spoons in a drawer, and as he slipped away into sleep, Kelly was planning her future. She'd go with him to New Orleans, but only for a trial period. She was too wise to expect romance to last for ever, and this was certainly romantic. No, she'd keep her options open at the Falcon Bookshop, but enjoy herself with Jake at the same time, share in his adventures, possibly dare to fall in love.

Yet a part of her would always remain heart-whole, an independent woman who followed her own destiny.

Wicked Ways

THE X LIBRIS READERS SURVEY

We hope you will take a moment to fill out this questionnaire and tell us more about what you want to read – and how we can provide it!

1. About you . . .

A)   Male   Female

B)   Under 21   41-50
        21-30   51-60
        31-40   Over 60

C)   Occupation_____

D)   Annual household income:
        under £10,000   £31-40,000
        £11-20,000   £41-50,000
        £21-30,000   Over £50,000

E)   At what age did you leave full-time education?

        16 or younger   20 or older
        17-19   still in education

2. About X Libris . . .

A)   How did you acquire this book?

        I bought it myself
        I borrowed/found it
        Someone else bought it for me

B)   How did you find out about X Libris books?

        in a shop
        in a magazine
        other _____

C)   Please tick any statements you agree with:

        I would feel more comfortable about buying X Libris books if the covers were less explicit

        I wish the covers of X Libris books were more explicit

        I think X Libris covers are just right

        If you could design your own X Libris cover, how would it look?

D)   Do you read X Libris books in public places (for example, on trains, at bus stops, etc.)?

        Yes   No